THE MYSTERY OF THE
CASTAWAY CHILDREN

The TRIXIE BELDEN Series

THE MYSTERY OF THE CASTAWAY CHILDREN

By Kathryn Kenny

A GOLDEN BOOK • NEW YORK

Western Publishing Company, Inc., Racine, Wisconsin 53404

CONTENTS

THE MYSTERY OF THE CASTAWAY CHILDREN

"It's Not a Skunk" • 1

Thump. Thump.

Pause.

"Go get it, Reddy!"

"Woof!"

Thump.

Inside the hot kitchen, Trixie Belden brushed the damp curls off her forehead as she finished up the last of the dinner dishes. The noise of her little brother Bobby throwing his ball against the side of the house was less than soothing. Apparently Reddy, the Beldens' Irish setter, was the outfielder. *Why is it always my turn to do the dishes on the muggiest nights of the summer?* Trixie thought irritably.

She wasn't the only Belden affected by the heat. She could hear her parents' conversation out on the porch, and both of them sounded rather testy.

"Peter," Trixie heard her mother say, "can't you play catch with Bobby until Brian and Mart come back with the ice cream? He's trampling my petunias."

Peter Belden had been trying to tell his wife about his day at work, but he stopped long enough to call, "Take it easy, Bobby. Windows cost money."

Trixie heard the creak of the porch swing as her father eased himself onto it. "Anyway," he went on, "I feel sorry for David Dodge. He came into the bank again several weeks ago to inquire about another loan, but we couldn't see our way clear to let him have any more money. Now he's having to auction off his property on Saw Mill River."

"Isn't his wife one of the Jacksons? Surely their credit is good," Mrs. Belden objected.

"They're both from families that have been in the area a long time," Mr. Belden replied, "but

14

that's not what establishes a good credit rating anymore, Helen. It's whether you pay your bills promptly that counts. This man Dodge is up to his ears in debt. He buys things he can't afford, and he uses credit cards like they're going out of style. When he runs short of ready cash, he borrows from the nearest friend and signs an IOU."

"What's wrong with that?" Mrs. Belden asked. "Credit cards aren't exactly dishonest."

"David Dodge isn't dishonest," Mr. Belden sighed. "He's careless. He's convinced he can pay, but he hasn't got any sense when it comes to money. He just plain indulges his family without counting the cost."

No wonder her father sounded disapproving, thought Trixie. His job at the First National Bank in Sleepyside taught him to respect money management and credit rating. He handled large sums of other people's money, while his own family lived in comfortable yet moderate circumstances on Crabapple Farm.

Trixie's thoughts drifted to a few indulgences she wouldn't mind having at Crabapple Farm. Central air conditioning, for a start. An electric dishwasher, too. Gleeps! She knew better than to ask for a dishwasher, though. Someone would be bound to tell her, "Who needs one? We have you!"

The trouble was that housework was not one of Trixie's passions. On the other hand, she loved the farm. Sharing the work was the price each Belden paid for living a quiet, uncluttered life. Trixie had only to glance out the window over the kitchen sink to see gardens and orchard, fields and lawn. She felt sorry for the family of that man her father was talking about. Evidently they had a place over on Saw Mill River, between the Hudson River and White Plains. It would be painful to have to give that up.

Despite the cloud blanket trapping heat in the hollow where the farm lay, Trixie could think of no place she'd rather be on this sweltering August night. Just the same . . . she'd be the last to complain if the family splurged on an electric dishwasher.

Trixie frowned to herself as she wiped the counters clean. "I'll climb the walls if it doesn't rain pretty soon," she muttered.

Finally she had the kitchen as spotless as she could make it, and she headed for the porch to join her parents. Plopping herself down on the steps, she inhaled the cooler air and shoved her mop of short sandy curls up from her hot neck.

Peter Belden had not taken his wife's suggestion to play with Bobby, who had moved his ball game to the wall of the garden shed in the backyard. Each time his ball dropped into the grass, grasshoppers whirred in protest. Robins were raising the last brood of the season in the maple tree by the doghouse. Disturbed by the weather, they sang their loudest. Trixie found the sound vaguely annoying. As she watched the cloud mass hanging over the Catskills, she heard the first rumble of thunder.

"Better watch out," she called to Bobby. "The Dunderberg goblin will get you."

Bobby had abandoned that legend with his baby food. He wasn't interested in the bumpy, lumpy fellow who sat on Dunderberg's peak and shouted to the winds through his speaking trumpet. "You 'rupted," yelled Bobby. "Now I can't hear it!"

"Hear what?" Trixie called back.

"I don't know. Something I heard."

"What did it sound like? A person? An animal?" Anything mysterious, large or small, immediately brought questions to Trixie's mind,

17

even on a hot night like this.

As usual, her six-year-old brother took his time while he considered Trixie's questions. He thumped his ball into his mitt as he thought. Evidently believing the game to be over, Reddy wandered off toward his doghouse. There he sniffed about, backed away, and sat staring at the shelter as if contemplating a remodeling job.

"Well?" Trixie prompted.

Trixie's temper was on a short fuse, but Bobby's was on an even shorter one. "I don't know!" he flared. "A kind of squeak, maybe. It mewed."

"Where did the sound come from?"

"I don't know that either," Bobby said flatly.

"Fine detective you'd make!" Trixie snorted.

Bobby, used to Trixie's mercurial disposition, paid no attention to her outburst. "I thought it was in the woods," he went on. "Then it moved closer. It sounded like—"

Trixie leaned forward.

Bobby shook his round, blond head. "No, it couldn't be."

Suddenly Trixie realized that Bobby was sincerely puzzled. What in the world could he have heard? Before she could question him further, the air seemed to shift, and the long-awaited rain came pouring down in sheets.

At the same time, both Trixie and Bobby whooped, "Let's get wet!"

Bobby threw his mitt onto the porch, and Trixie scampered down the steps. Together they dashed around the corner of the house to the front yard, which sloped toward the lane. Great big drops spattered the leaves of oaks and maples and sent up little dust puffs from the dry patches on the lawn. Trixie and Bobby kicked off their sneakers and ran through the grass, singing as much as they could remember of "Singin' in the Rain."

Soon it was raining so hard that puddles formed in the lane. Bubbles floated, only to burst when struck by raindrops. Bobby yanked off his T-shirt and splashed from puddle to puddle.

Trixie chased him, shouting, "Dad! Moms! Come and play with us!"

Peter Belden called back, "For two cents, I'd take you up on that."

Trixie searched the pockets of her shorts. "You're safe, Dad!" she yelled.

"Oh, no, you're not," Bobby said. He sprinted over to the porch to plop two pennies into his father's hand.

"Come on, Bobby, have a heart," Mr. Belden begged.

"Race you to the mailbox!" urged Trixie.

"Peter, you wouldn't," Mrs. Belden protested, laughing.

"If they can do it, I suppose their father might as well," he defended himself as he handed his watch to his wife.

Mrs. Belden shook her head in amusement as the trio raced down the lane, shouting their pleasure at the change of weather. Reddy decided to race in the opposite direction—toward the porch, where he showered Mrs. Belden with rain spray. She was frantically pushing him away from her when the racers returned. A soggy but happy group of Beldens watched from the porch while the rain tapered to sprinkles.

The summer storm was over by the time Brian and Mart returned with an ice-cream treat from Mr. Lytell's store. Trixie smacked her lips as her older brothers hopped out of Brian's jalopy and made their way around the puddles toward the porch. When the boys reached the steps, they stopped short at the sight of the rest of their family, especially their father.

Mr. Belden was seldom careless in his appearance, yet there he sat, white shirt clinging to his chest and black hair dripping water down his neck. Whenever he moved his feet, water squished from his shoes. And he was *smiling*.

Mart was the first to express his amazement. "Such a state of bedewed dishevelment is not unheard of regarding our callow siblings, lamentable though it may be. But our sire?" Mart raised an eyebrow at Brian. "Methinks he has been led astray."

"I strayed him for two cents," Bobby declared.

"Money talks," chuckled Brian.

"Jeepers, who wants to talk?" broke in Trixie. "Let's get at that ice cream!"

Her family agreed, and in a matter of minutes, they all polished off their desserts.

"There. I heard it again," said Bobby abruptly.

"Sounds like a baby crying," commented Brian.

"That's what I thought," Bobby said.

"Impossible," Mart scoffed. "Except for Di Lynch's twin brothers and sisters, you're the youngest child in the area."

"That's what it sounds like," insisted Bobby. "A scared baby."

By then, Trixie was taking her little brother

21

seriously. "What else would sound like a baby?" she wondered aloud. "A mockingbird, maybe? It copycats sound."

"Babies sound most like babies," said Bobby.

Brian tousled Bobby's fair hair. "True, but it's just been pointed out that there are no babies to be heard around here."

"The 'cat' in Catskill comes from *catamount*," recalled Mrs. Belden. "Could the storm have driven one in from Wheelers' game preserve?" Her hand moved instinctively toward Bobby's shoulders.

"Possible, but I doubt it," Mr. Belden said. He stood up and reached for the screen door. "I'm off for a shower. Anybody using water at the same time had better be sure *she* doesn't use all the hot water." Pretending to scowl darkly, he squished into the house.

"Who'd want hot water on a night like this?" Bobby asked sensibly.

"Or any water, period," added Trixie. "I'm perfectly comfortable just the way I am."

"Who am I to mention that you're perfectly unkempt, too," teased Mart.

"You're my almost twin," retorted Trixie, "so you'd better watch what you say about me."

Mart grimaced, then reached for a strand of Trixie's sandy curls. "With this hair, you can just shake yourself dry, like Reddy," he taunted.

"Thanks for the tip," said Trixie, and she leaned over to Mart to do just that.

Mart scooted to safety, and Mrs. Belden laughed. "I'm afraid I have to side with Mart," she said. "You're *all* going to need showers."

She went inside to check on the towel supply, while the younger Beldens remained on the porch to enjoy the breeze that had followed the rain.

Trixie and Mart were about to resume their friendly bickering, when a prolonged, thin wail arose. Reddy, resting beside Trixie, perked up his ears. After a few tail thumps, the dog padded to the edge of the porch. The sound stopped as abruptly as it had begun, yet Reddy jumped from the porch, sniffing the air. Trixie got up to follow him, while Mart and Brian exchanged glances behind her. Curiosity might as well have been Trixie's middle name.

She saw Reddy approaching his doghouse. When he reached the opening, he ducked his head, then backed away. Trixie was puzzled when the setter made a few uncertain circles around his own house, peered in, then sat down.

Then she remembered that this was copper-head country. Snakes were one of the few things that really made Trixie nervous. She knew Reddy would have sense enough to respect squatter's rights if a copperhead had moved into his house. So she, too, stayed a safe distance from the low, unpainted shelter. Even from there, she could see a white mass that contrasted with the dim interior of the house. What could that be? Reddy slept on an old rug on a bed of straw. The rug had long since lost most of its color. It wasn't white, and it never had been.

Frowning, she returned to the porch, where her three brothers looked up at her expectantly.

"What's with our capricious canine?" inquired Mart.

"I couldn't get close enough to find anything," Trixie admitted. "Reddy wouldn't go inside his own doghouse, so I didn't go near it, either."

"Admirable caution," cheered Mart lazily.

Brian took a closer look at his sister's concerned face and rose from the porch swing. "I'll get the pitchfork and see what's moved in," he said.

Trixie followed Brian to the backyard and

waited for him to bring a pitchfork from the garden shed.

"See? Reddy isn't afraid," she pointed out. "He just won't go in."

"Maybe it's a skunk," Brian said without enthusiasm. "Well, let's get this over with." He strode toward the doghouse, pitchfork ready for action. Reddy turned his sleek red head in the direction of his home.

Trixie was prepared for anything, but still she couldn't believe it when Brian suddenly dropped his pitchfork and actually stretched his arms inside the doghouse. He was down on his knees, paying no attention to the mud. Trixie gasped with surprise as Brian started to rise. He was lifting a white bundle from Reddy's straw bed and holding it against his chest. He turned to Trixie, his face blank with astonishment.

"It's—it's not a skunk" was all Brian could manage to say.

Trixie came near and took a good look at the bundle. "Yipes!" she exclaimed softly. "It's not a snake, either!"

Before she could gather her wits about her to fire questions at Brian, he was taking long steps in the direction of the porch. Trixie raced to

25

catch up. Reddy was close at her heels.

As the group neared the porch, Bobby and Mart stopped their playful wrestling long enough for Mart to call, "Snakes aren't allowed on the porch." Then he did a double take. "Is th-that what I think it is?" he gulped.

"It is!" crowed Bobby. "It's a real, live baby!"

Brian lowered his arms to allow Bobby to uncover the baby's face. Four young Beldens watched a soft pink mouth blow till a bubble formed. Blue eyes stared out of a dirty face, then squeezed shut. A fretful whimper was quickly stilled when Brian lifted the tiny body against his shoulder.

"I told you a baby sounds most like a baby," Bobby declared, not in the least taken aback.

Mart, still in a state of shock, touched the little blanket, muddy from when Brian had pulled the baby out of the doghouse. "Blanket . . . wet . . ." he muttered.

Trixie sprang into action. Up the steps she leaped, crossing the porch in two bounds and flinging open the door. "Moms!" she shouted. "MOTHER!"

Mrs. Belden hurried down the stairs and into the hall. When she was called "Mother" instead of "Moms," there was usually an emergency. "What's wrong, Trixie?"

Trixie held the door open and ushered her mother out onto the porch. Mrs. Belden looked bewildered as Brian held out his tiny charge toward her. "We found something, uh, out of the ordinary," he told her.

"That can't be—" Mrs. Belden whispered.

"It's a baby, all right," said Bobby matter-of-factly.

The minute Mrs. Belden's hands touched the blanket, she was in command of the situation. "Trixie, bring dry towels—the softest you can find," she ordered. "And get that baby oil you use for suntan lotion. Mart, call Mrs. Lynch to see if she can spare some baby clothes. Brian, you scald milk."

"What proportion of corn syrup?" Brian asked on his way inside.

Already halfway up the stairs, Trixie glanced back, startled by Brian's question. *Well, why wouldn't Brian know about baby food?* she asked herself. *He has three younger siblings, and he is the doctor-to-be around here.*

Freshly showered and dressed in clean, dry clothes, Mr. Belden ran into Trixie in the upstairs hall. "What's all the rumpus?" he asked.

At a loss for an explanation, Trixie blurted, "We have a new baby!" Then she hurried to fetch the towels, leaving her father to gaze after her, openmouthed.

Minutes later, a sober Belden family gathered around the kitchen table. Mrs. Belden was bathing the tiny boy, who shuddered with nervousness, temperature change, and hunger. "Poor baby, I wonder how you got so dirty," she crooned. "You're too hungry and tired to even cry."

"That's just when I do cry," Bobby confessed.

"Don't we know," Trixie sighed.

Brian made the formula by his mother's directions and cooled it to suit himself. Then he trickled milk from the tip of a spoon into the baby's mouth. "I know he's swallowing too much air," Brian worried.

"He'll burp," Bobby surmised.

"How old is he?" Mart was still so flabbergasted that he forgot to use the longest words in the dictionary.

Mrs. Belden thought for a moment. "He weighs about twelve pounds. If his birth weight was an average six pounds and he gained at the regular rate of eight ounces a week, a weight of twelve pounds would indicate an age of three months. Don't you think that's about right, Peter?" She turned toward Mr. Belden. "Peter, have you been listening to a word I've said?"

Mr. Belden shifted his gaze to his wife. "But, Helen . . . a *baby?*" he asked weakly.

Elastic Walls · 2

SOON, IN RESPONSE TO Mart's telephone call, the Belden kitchen was crowded with new arrivals. Di Lynch had brought with her not only a package of baby clothes, but also Honey Wheeler and Jim Frayne.

Di had two sets of twins at her house. Mrs. Lynch had gathered up a wardrobe for the newcomer simply by opening dresser drawers in a storage room. As she handed the package to Mrs. Belden, Di said, "My mother said to tell you that if she's omitted something essential, I'll call our butler to drive over and drop it off. She also said to tell you, 'Congratulations!' "

"I'm sure she thought of everything," Mrs. Belden said, hastily sorting out a change of clothing for the baby. "Thank you!"

Honey, Trixie's best friend and her partner in mystery-solving, set down a grocery sack, from which she took cans of formula and packages of disposable bottles and diapers. "When Mart called, Jim and I were at the Lynches'," she explained. "Jim drove us straight to Mr. Lytell's store for the formula. We didn't think you'd have any. Oh, Trixie, isn't this exciting? The Belden-Wheeler Detective Agency has found a lot of lost articles, but never a baby before!" She turned to Mrs. Belden. "How much formula do I put in this bottle?"

"Here, let me help you," Brian offered. At the kitchen counter, the two bent to the important task of serving the waif's first full-fledged meal at the farm.

Mrs. Belden dressed the baby while Mart went to the laundry room for the clothes basket. Bobby ran upstairs and returned with his own soft blanket to be used as a mattress. Honey handed the bottle to Brian, who took charge of the feeding. At once the infant set to work.

31

For a moment, the watchers were so quiet that they could hear the occasional intake of air and smack of lips.

"The boy's a bottomless pit," Mart commented in amazement.

"Mart, I think you've met your match," Brian said dryly.

Freckle-faced Jim Frayne, Honey's adopted brother, shook his head in wonder. "I'd forgotten babies were that small."

Already Bobby felt possessive. "He's not finished yet. See? No hair and no teeth!"

Brian took the half-emptied bottle from the baby.

"Please, may I burp him?" Trixie asked.

"Don't drop him," warned Bobby, "and don't get him wet again."

"I'm dry now," Trixie assured him. She raised the towel-wrapped baby to her shoulder and patted him carefully. She was so thrilled that she didn't even flinch when warm milk trickled onto her shoulder.

"Maybe it's time to relinquish the cherub," Mark teased gently, "before he develops an allergy to schoolgirl shamuses!"

Trixie ignored him and continued her patting.

How could anyone abandon this sweet creature? she thought.

Pretty Di felt left out. "Let me hold him," she begged.

"He needs rest," Mrs. Belden decided. "Di, you and Mart may carry that basket to the guest room. With the door open, we'll be able to hear him if he cries."

The guest room was dimly lighted. Even though it was a hot August night, Trixie rushed ahead of Di and Mart to find a spot where the baby wouldn't be bothered by a draft. Cautiously, Di and Mart set the basket down where Trixie indicated. Leaving the door ajar, the three tiptoed from the room.

In the kitchen, they found family and friends enjoying fruit punch and cookies and discussing the baby.

"Trixie, tell us all about it!" Honey demanded. "I never heard of anything so mysterious in my whole life."

At the word "mysterious," Trixie's round blue eyes began to shimmer. She and Honey constantly found themselves involved in mysteries. They had solved so many of them that they were planning to form their own detective agency eventually. In their sleuthing, they usually had the loyal support of the Bob-Whites of the Glen, a club that, besides Trixie and Honey, included Di, Jim, Brian, and Mart. The seventh member, Dan Mangan, was frequently too busy with other responsibilities to take part in the mysteries. Mysteries just seemed to drop into Trixie's and Honey's lives as if by a miracle . . . like this baby.

Trixie jumped up and rummaged through the baby's things.

"Did my mother forget something?" Di asked.

"I'm looking for clues," Trixie explained. "But there aren't many. There's a diaper, a blanket, and a knitted shirt—not much to go on."

"That blanket and shirt are of very good quality," observed Di.

"Maybe there's a note in the doghouse," Mart suggested.

"The *what?*" Di squeaked.

"Did you say *doghouse?*" Honey put in.

"That's where we found him," Brian answered. He was already on his way out of the kitchen. Soon he came back to report that there was no note, and that the heavy rain had washed away all tracks except his own.

"How in the world did you know he was there?" gasped Honey.

"I heard him first," Bobby reported. "He kind of mewed. You know, like a kitten."

"When did you first hear him?" asked Di.

"Before the rain," Bobby replied.

Jim looked upset. "Who would shove a baby into a doghouse and leave him alone in the middle of a storm?"

Honey's hazel eyes welled with sympathetic tears. "And why?" she cried.

Inside Trixie's skull, the wheels were spinning. A living, breathing mystery lay sleeping in their house. Who was this tiny boy? Who had failed to protect him? What drama had been enacted in their backyard earlier that evening? Somehow, Trixie knew she would discover answers for those questions.

Trixie had been crumbling a cookie, totally out of contact with family and friends. She looked up to meet her father's dark eyes.

Mr. Belden refilled his punch glass. His fingers drummed the tabletop. "I recognize the symptoms," he sighed. "You're about to solve the kidnapping case of the century and get your name in the headlines of *The New York Times*.

Trixie, I must insist we go to the police at once. A human life is involved. We can't take a chance on a haphazard search."

"Haphazard!" Trixie's temper blazed.

Mr. Belden raised one hand for silence. "Hear me out, Beatrix."

"Wow," Bobby breathed. "That's Trixie's company name, same as mine is Robert."

Mr. Belden nodded and went on. "Brian, since you're the one who found the baby, you're the logical one to call the Sleepyside police."

Brian crossed the kitchen to the phone, while Trixie exchanged crestfallen glances with Honey. As determined as she'd been to take on this case for herself, Trixie knew, deep down, that her father was right.

Brian cleared his throat. "This is Brian Belden, and I wish to report—oh, Sergeant Molinson!"

Eye contact united the Bob-Whites. Although Sergeant Molinson usually ended up expressing reluctant appreciation for their efforts in solving crimes, his first reaction was always impatience with the young people's "interference" with police business.

"Sir, have you a report of a missing child?" Brian asked. "We've found an abandoned baby."

Brian turned to the others to report, "He's checking." Then he muttered, "Yes, sir," several times. Finally he turned to his parents. "The sergeant says he has to contact the FBI, in case there's a kidnapping involved. That's a federal crime. Also, he thinks it will take a few hours to get the official wheels rolling. Is it all right if I say we're willing to give the baby lodging till then?"

"Of course," said Mrs. Belden.

"If we're going to have to keep the baby more than a day or two," Brian continued, "the county will send a social worker tomorrow to investigate us. And the sergeant will be here tomorrow morning for the same purpose."

"Investigate *us?*" Trixie gasped. That was a switch.

After Brian had finished his conversation and rejoined the group around the polished maple table, Di spoke up. "Mrs. Belden, if your house is too crowded, I'm sure we could care for the baby in our nursery. After all, with two sets of twins and a nurse for each pair, we're certainly equipped for it, and I know my parents wouldn't mind."

Then Honey offered the hospitality of Manor

House, the Wheeler mansion. "Miss Trask would fit that baby into her schedule in no time at all," she insisted. Miss Trask managed Manor House, but still had time to be a friend to her young charges, Jim and Honey.

Bobby looked distressed. "Moms! Dad! There's plenty of room in our house, isn't there?"

Mrs. Belden smiled at the two girls. "Thank you for offering, but we'll manage. These walls are elastic. There's always room for one more at Crabapple Farm, isn't there, Peter?"

Peter Belden agreed, though a trace of bewilderment still lingered in his eyes.

Trixie turned to Jim, her copresident of the Bob-Whites. "Even though Dan's patrolling the game preserve tonight and won't be able to come, I think we should have a club meeting now."

"If you say so," Jim answered. "We can fill Dan in later. By the way, what happened to you? Get dumped in a rain barrel?"

"The precipitation drove her to distraction," Mart remarked. "We're applying for federal flood control funds tomorrow."

Trixie glanced down at the clothing that had dried on her warm skin. Her hair was still damp, and her bare legs and feet were splotched with dried mud. "I forgot to take my bath," she giggled. "Let's meet on the front porch."

Bobby had wisely refrained from mentioning baths. "Let me come, too," he suggested.

Mr. Belden glanced outside at the dark sky. "I think you have a previous engagement with the tub and your bed, son."

Bobby poked out his lower lip, but he spoiled the effect by yawning. "I heard that baby first," he began. "I think I should stay up and talk about it some more."

"And I think you should go to bed," his mother said.

"I might 'member something I thought I forgot," Bobby said slyly.

"Then you think about it and tell us in the morning. Scoot!" Mr. Belden ordered.

Stalling for time, Bobby said good night to each person in the room, then asked, "Can I say 'night to the baby?"

"*May* I," Mart corrected. Words were Mart's love.

"Sure, you, too," said Bobby with a wave of his arm.

Mr. Belden threw up his hands, and one by

one, the group tiptoed into the guest room for a last peek at the sleeping infant.

Who are you? Trixie asked him silently. *How long will we be able to keep you?*

Once the Bob-Whites were comfortably seated on the front porch, Trixie called the meeting to order. Although the rain had stopped, only a few stars managed to elude the cloud blanket. It was pleasantly dark. Grass and flowers smelled clean and fresh. Trixie felt full of energy, as though all the nervous crankiness of the day had been washed away.

Brian was the first to speak. "Moms already has her hands full. I think we owe it to her to arrange some kind of schedule, in case the baby is here through tomorrow. To be on the safe side, he should be fed every four hours, and that's only part of his care."

"An exemplary diet schedule" was Mart's comment. At fifteen, growing fast, he was always hungry.

"I'll share the work," said Honey, and Di was quick to agree.

"I, for one, could really use the experience of caring for an infant," Brian put in. "Besides . . ."

"You feel, if not exactly paternal, at least

fraternal," Mart finished for him.

"Right," Brian said.

"Me, too," Mart admitted.

"If this is a learning experience, I can use it, too," Jim said.

"Good!" Trixie said. "Then it's unanimous to share the baby's care?"

"Yes!" was the response of the Bob-Whites. Part of the club's function was to help people in need of help, and there couldn't be anyone more helpless than a tiny baby.

"Until we know who he is, he kind of belongs to us," Di mused. "Shouldn't he have a name? We can't keep calling that baby 'he' and 'it.' "

"Such an appellation is awkward," Mart agreed.

"If we didn't already have a Bobby, we could name him Bob White," Honey said.

"We don't have a Clancy," Mart said impishly.

"Nobody names a three-month-old baby Clancy!" Di exclaimed.

"I should hope not," Mart told her. "Most of the Clancys I know were named months earlier than that."

"What about Moses?" Jim asked.

The whole group hooted.

41

"Moses was hidden in a basket and pulled out of the Nile River," Jim argued. "This little guy was pulled out of Reddy's doghouse in the rain."

"We could call him Mo," suggested Honey.

Di, who enjoyed being a hostess, spoke up next. "Let's have a welcoming party for Moses Bob-White, with a naming ceremony. We could have arks for favors!"

"Wrong patriarch—that was Noah," Mart teased. "But you're on the right track. We could decorate with bulrushes."

"I never did find out what a bulrush was," Di said plaintively.

"Never mind," Mart said. "You have black hair and violet eyes."

The rest of the group didn't see what that had to do with bulrushes, but Di seemed satisfied.

"All in favor of Moses Bob-White?" Trixie inquired.

The vote was unanimous again, and Brian pointed out that it was almost ten o'clock.

"So?" Honey asked.

"Six, ten, two, six, ten, two," Brian said. "That's Mo's schedule."

"Dibs on feeding Mo before Jim takes us home," Di called.

"I'll take two," Brian offered. "I'll want to check to see if he has a cold."

"Six for me," Mart said. "I'm certain our sister will still be somnolent."

"Whatever that is, I won't be," retorted Trixie. "You'll need help. Make that six for *us*."

Later that night, Trixie lay awake for some time, racking her brain over Moses and where he might have come from. A few minutes' walk in any direction from this farm placed one in the wilderness. Then, just barely out of sight was a great spider web of bridges, tunnels, parkways and turnpikes, state highways and county roads, country lanes and bridle trails, footpaths and animal traces. When you added the air lanes, railroads, and canal and river traffic of New York City, it was possible to say that the world's traffic flowed past Crabapple Farm.

Thinking of the millions of people who traveled on this traffic pattern every day, Trixie was overwhelmed by the size of the mystery she faced. Moses could have come from Sleepyside-on-the-Hudson, or Beulah, North Dakota, or Ocean Beach, California. He might have come from any place in the whole wide world.

Yet there he was, sleeping in the Belden

clothes basket. Was he left by a starving young mother who could no longer take care of him? Was he unloved and unwanted? Had he been kidnapped and abandoned for some reason? Was someone out there right now in the wet dark, watching the house? If that someone did care what happened to the baby, what would that person do when the police came?

Police!

"I forgot about Sergeant Molinson," Trixie mumbled to herself. He would arrive early. Well, then there was one person who was going to get up even earlier.

Trixie set her alarm clock.

Batter Is Pancakes · 3

AT FIVE-THIRTY, Trixie was dressed and quietly slipping from the house. Her first stop was at the doghouse.

Reddy was less prepared to face the day than was Trixie. He stirred and yawned, until finally she was able to persuade him to come out.

Trixie patted around the edges of Reddy's rug, but Brian's search had been thorough. There was no ransom note, no good-bye letter, not even an extra piece of clothing or a soft toy—nothing that might be traced.

Trixie stood up, looked about, and informed

Reddy, "Unless someone brought Moses through the raspberry patch, he must have used the bike path." This trail ran downhill from the Manor House stables. After crossing the farm, the path roughly paralleled Glen Road all the way to Glen Road Inn.

Reddy looked unimpressed, and Trixie headed alone into the woods, which were cool and clean after the rain. She could smell the grass she stepped on and could see the rainbow jewels in the wet, sunlit spider webs. On such a heart-lifting morning, nothing should be wrong with the world. Yet something was very wrong for one little boy. Soberly Trixie studied the earth she walked on.

She saw nothing unusual, just a path chopped by horses' hoofprints. Because of the daily exercising of all the horses in the Wheeler stables, the crisscrossing trails on the game preserve were naturally marked with myriad prints. There was also Mr. Lytell, who often rode slowpokey old Belle on these grounds. Dan saved time by riding Spartan when he ran errands for Regan, the Wheelers' groom, and Mr. Maypenny, the Wheelers' gamekeeper. Even Di's palomino, Sunny, spent much time on Wheeler land. All of these animals were loved and given the care one would give a human.

Then—what was this horseshoe doing in the middle of the path?

Concerned, Trixie picked the shoe up. This was a bicycle trail as well as a bridle path. An obstacle like that could cause a bad spill if one were going full speed down the hill. And, when coming down this hill from the Wheeler stables, there were only two bicycle speeds—fast and faster. Who would have been so careless?

Trixie was still carrying the mud-caked shoe as she neared the Wheeler stables, continuing her search for clues. She could hear men's voices and the movement and whickering of animals being fed. Regan always got an early start in his conscientious grooming of the horses. As Trixie got closer, she caught sight through a window of a red head bent over some early-morning task. Up here on the hill lived three red-haired men: Matthew Wheeler himself, Jim Frayne, and Regan. Trixie hoped that was Jim she saw.

It was. Trixie forgot that her sneakered feet would give Jim no warning of her presence. She was only a few feet away from him when he noticed her and immediately dropped the towel

47

he'd been wiping his hands on.

"Yikes!" he exclaimed. "Where'd you come from? And what brings you here so early?"

"Hi!" Trixie blurted. Then she saw the clock near the tack room door. "Oh, jeepers, I lost track of the time. Gotta go!" She tossed the iron horseshoe onto a shelf and started racing back down the hill.

A minute later, Jim came whizzing behind her on his bicycle. As he caught up, he called, "Even though I'm not wild about your entrances and exits this morning, I'll give you a ride home if you give me breakfast."

"It's a deal," Trixie agreed.

Balancing on Jim's handlebars, Trixie enjoyed the cool morning air that struck her face. As Jim coasted down the steep, twisting path, trees and boulders flashed by. They came to the spot where she had picked up the horseshoe. Had Jim hit it at this speed, they would have had a terrible accident. She pointed with her head and said, "That's where I found it."

Jim leaned forward. "Found what?"

"The horseshoe. Who lost it? Not Susie, I hope." Susie was the small black mare Trixie loved to ride, even though the beautiful animal really belonged to Miss Trask.

"All our horses' shoes are on tight this morning," answered Jim. "I checked them myself."

"I've been searching the path for clues about Moses' arrival," Trixie explained.

"Have you considered that he might have been brought on a motorcycle?" Jim inquired.

Trixie was thoughtful. "You're right—the baby could have ridden in the sidecar."

"The only thing is, we haven't seen any tire marks," said Jim, bringing the bike to a halt as they came near the gate behind the doghouse.

Inside the Belden house, the day had already begun. Mrs. Belden was bustling about the kitchen, which was filled with the good smells of bacon and coffee. She greeted Trixie with a look of amusement.

"The baby seems to have gotten everyone up on the early side this morning," chuckled Mrs. Belden. "Even my daughter." She called to Bobby, "Set another plate. Jim is having breakfast with us." With a welcoming twinkle at Jim, she asked, "You are, aren't you?" She turned back to Trixie. "Mart's on cloud nine. He's so positive you're fast asleep that he's taking charge of the baby."

49

"That double crosser," fumed Trixie.

"Mart didn't drop him, or stick him with pins, or anything bad," Bobby declared. "Yet," he added darkly.

Trixie rushed into the guest room to see for herself. She found Mart in full control, so intent on dressing Moses that he was not aware Trixie had come in until she spoke.

At the sight of the child, Trixie forgot her petty irritation. "He's so little, so thin," she whispered tenderly.

"I know," her brother answered soberly. "Last night, I thought he was just very young and very small, but this morning . . ."

"He looks like a half-starved little bird!" Trixie winked back tears.

During the previous night's excitement, no one had really studied the tired baby. In the early morning sunlight, Trixie was shocked to see that Moses was smaller than the doll she used to hang by ribbon straps beside her dressing table. A little fuzz of dark hair grew above his ears and on the top of his head, but it was worn to the skin on the back of his head.

"Oh, my gosh, Mart!" Trixie cried softly. "He— he has bruises! And his hands—they're just like little bird claws," she moaned.

Bobby entered the room and announced, "His feet, too. And you know what, Trixie? One foot is dirty, and Mart can't get it clean."

"Tar," Mart said briefly. "And some kind of machine oil, but I got that off." Carefully he moved Moses' bony legs. "See these abrasions? Brian thinks he must have had a fall several days ago, but I don't think he fell. Look—the bruises are just under his arms and on his stomach."

Trixie sank down on the bed, weak with sudden anger. "Oh, Mart, do you think someone has actually b-battered Moses?"

"Batter is pancakes," said Bobby, puzzled.

"Batter also means to beat more than once," his brother explained quietly. "Violent abuse and neglect are now the largest causes of death among American children."

Bobby released a shivering sigh. "Then I'm glad somebody quit battering up Moses and stuck him in our doghouse."

"What can be done, legally, about child abuse?" Trixie asked her brother.

Mart was the family clown, but he had a well-stocked mind. It didn't surprise Trixie that he was able to tell her about the laws that required

51

certain professionals to report abuse and encouraged citizens to report suspected neglect.

Trixie clenched her hands. "I simply have to find the—the so-called person who let these things happen to Moses."

"I'll help you," Mart said simply. Usually he teased Trixie mercilessly about her mysteries, but this case had obviously aroused his sympathetic concern.

"Has Moms started the laundry?" Trixie asked abruptly.

"Not that I know of."

Trixie hurried to the laundry room. She took a second look at the pitifully small heap of dirty clothing that had been tossed into the hamper. This time she noticed that the diaper had been fashioned from a T-shirt. It felt as if it had been washed without soap. The blanket and knitted shirt were soft, but both were dirt-smudged. When she turned the shirt inside out to check once more for a tag, she found a dried leaf she had missed before. She'd have to ask Mart, the future agriculturist, to identify it. She placed the baby clothing back in the hamper and headed once more toward the guest room. She knew her mother wouldn't wash the things

52

until Sergeant Molinson had examined them.

By now, Brian was trying to take command of the guest-room nursery, but it was Mart who cradled Moses in his arms and gave the baby the feeding he had promised. Trixie didn't try to interfere. She watched, her thoughts racing.

She was familiar with the nursery routine in the Lynch mansion. Although they were no longer infants, Trixie remembered how those privileged Lynch babies had squirmed with energy. They had kicked and snatched and howled.

Moses did none of those things. He moved feebly. Plainly he was hungry, but sucking seemed to tire his throat and tongue. He rested often, fretted, and tried again. Once his eyes focused on Trixie. They seemed sad and filled with pain.

"Is he sick, Brian?" Trixie faltered.

"Just weak, I think. Moms is going to ask the investigator to see about a thorough checkup."

Moses dozed off without finishing his bottle. Mart covered him up, Brian left the door ajar, and the group returned to the kitchen. Trixie showed Mart the leaf she had found.

"Alfalfa," Mart informed her.

"That's no help," muttered Trixie. Alfalfa meant Moses could have come from the country, and tar and machine oil meant he could have come from the city. How would she ever be able to narrow down the field?

As the Belden family and Jim were finishing breakfast, Sergeant Molinson tapped on the door and called through the screen, "Can you spare a cup of that good-smelling brew?"

"Come on in, Sergeant," Mr. Belden invited.

After the burly policeman had taken a sip of Mrs. Belden's coffee, he said gruffly, "This sure beats station-house ink, believe me."

"What have you turned up about the baby?" asked Brian.

The sergeant accepted a piece of buttered toast and replied, "South of here, a couple of boys are missing. I'm going to run over there this morning and see what's going on. I'll get a picture of them." He requested that all of them relate what they knew about the baby, then he cast a shrewd look at Trixie. "I presume you've made a thorough search for clues concerning the baby's identity?"

"Yes, sir," Trixie answered.

"Any objections if I go over the place again?"

Trixie reddened but shook her head. *As if he thinks he's going to find something I missed,* she fumed silently.

The sergeant opened a notebook and ambled into the yard, where he spent a long time pacing around and examining possible routes. Trixie looked smug when he, too, theorized that the woods path had been used.

"I found hoofprints and a horseshoe on the path," she told him.

The sergeant shrugged. "Who walks around here when it's just as easy to straddle a horse?" He closed his notebook with a snap. "I'll check the path to Glen Road Inn before I go to Saw Mill River."

Saw Mill River, Trixie thought. *Where have I heard that recently?*

After the sergeant had gone, Mary Goodley, a social worker from the county, arrived with her long list of questions. Mr. Belden had left for work, but everyone else stood in an interested circle while she examined Moses. Miss Goodley, a tall blond woman, agreed that Moses was pitifully thin. "I'll have a doctor sent out as soon as possible to check him over," she informed them. "He'll want to have a look at those abrasions, of course, but I notice that baby oil and an antiseptic have already been applied. Good thinking on someone's part."

Brian smiled faintly.

After inspecting the guest room, Miss Goodley sat down at the desk, by the window overlooking the rose garden Grandma Belden had planted years ago, to fill out her report.

"Sex, male. Name, unknown," she said aloud.

"Wrong," Bobby said. "His name's Moses Bob-White."

Miss Goodley fluttered a slim hand. "But I thought—"

"We named him, Miss Goodley," Trixie explained quickly.

"Moses Bob-White, you say?" Miss Goodley shook her long blond hair. Trixie was standing close enough to the social worker to see that she was careful to write the name with both quotation marks and question marks.

Miss Goodley looked over the rest of the house and talked to Mrs. Belden about feeding schedules, sunshine, and rest. "I'd limit his playtime till he's stronger," she decided. "But he obviously feels loved here, and that's the best medicine. I'm sure I can get approval for you to keep him another day or two, until the police have more leads about his identity."

Then she was gone, and the Belden family breathed a sigh of relief.

Jim was about to leave to finish his stable chores, when Honey burst in upon the group in the kitchen. "You're leaving me out!" she accused breathlessly.

"Since when do you get up at this hour, Sis?" Jim inquired.

"I wanted to see the baby being fed," Honey wailed.

"That was a long time ago. He's asleep again," Bobby told her. "Moses sleeps an awful lot."

"Look who's talking," Mart put in. "And, speaking of the passage of time, isn't it time that you 'tire yourself in suitable raiment for the exigencies of the day?"

"I'm not tired," Bobby said sturdily.

"I think he means get dressed," Trixie told Bobby, who needed just as much help as she did with Mart's outlandish language.

Honey begged for a peek at Moses, and Trixie led her to the guest room. The baby whimpered and moved restlessly in his sleep, kicking off the light coverlet.

"How did he get his stomach so dirty?" Honey whispered.

"Those are bruises," Trixie told her.

"Oh, no!" Honey looked horrified.

"Oh, yes!" Trixie said fiercely. "We simply have to find that baby's parents, Honey."

"But the police—" Honey began.

Trixie's blue eyes rounded with determination. "I'm going to give this case all my time." When Honey said nothing, Trixie amended, "Well, as much time as I can spare from helping with Moses, and of course, helping Moms, and keeping track of Bobby . . . and feeding the chickens—oh, jeepers! Do you realize there are forty old biddies out there cackling their heads off because I haven't fed them?"

"Come on, I'll help," said Honey, giving her friend a push.

"Gleeps, Honey," said Trixie as they were welcomed by the hungry chickens, "for someone who has a jillion servants and is as beautiful as you are, it's sure weird that you don't mind doing farm tasks."

Honey giggled. "Oh, Trixie, you're exaggerating again," she said. "I'm not beautiful, and I don't have a jillion servants. Besides, I'm sure even beautiful people like to help their friends."

That was certainly true in Honey's case, Trixie thought fondly. She'd earned her nickname for her golden brown hair and melting brown eyes, as well as for the genuine sweetness of her disposition. Honey and Di were both very pretty, but Honey was more practical.

Trixie knew herself to be both like and unlike Honey and Di. She was more impetuous than Honey, outdoorsy and healthy-looking rather than beautiful, and more practical than either of her wealthier friends. Trixie's grades were not as good as Honey's, but Di considered her a "brain." Trixie worked hard, not because she really liked to get her hands dirty, but because that was how it was, being a Belden of Crabapple Farm. She liked people and had an insatiable curiosity about the tangled lives they led.

Honey was very familiar with Trixie's curiosity. "What's our next step in finding Moses' parents?" she asked. "I'm sure you've got something up your sleeve."

"You'll see," promised Trixie.

One Iron Nail · 4

TRIXIE AND HONEY returned to the house after feeding the chickens to find Mrs. Belden sorting the laundry.

"I'll finish in here," she told Trixie, "while you make up the beds. Let's see . . . by that time, Moses will be awake. Bobby will be glad to just sit and talk to that baby. Oh, Di called to say she'll take the two o'clock feeding. Now, we'll have sandwiches for lunch, and everyone will make his own. My goodness," she sighed. "The day's just begun, and already I feel like it's slipping through my fingers!"

"You know you have all of our fingers to help you," said Trixie with more enthusiasm than she really felt. She was impatient to get to work on her new case, but she knew her chores came first.

"When do I get to feed Moses?" Honey asked.

"We'll take six o'clock," Trixie said hastily. "Now, let's get at those beds."

Trixie had no idea what clues she might find in the woods, but she had a feeling they'd be on that path. It was obvious that Moses would be cared for. Di would arrive well before two, of that Trixie was sure. Di loved children and never missed the chance to help with her own twin brothers and sisters. Trixie felt that she and Honey could give their best service by solving the mystery of Moses' identity.

While they worked, Trixie filled Honey in on the news of the morning. "All we really have to go on is that horseshoe," she finished.

"That's not much," Honey pointed out. "Are we done here?"

"Yes, believe it or not. Let's go!"

The woods were still wet, but the leaves were drying fast. Trixie and Honey saw at once that the sergeant had walked beside the path, not on it. The ground was cut by meandering rivulets.

In the low spots, water still moved sluggishly. Trixie was relieved to see that the sergeant didn't seem to have stooped to pick up any possible clues. He hadn't altered his steady pace alongside the trail.

"What are we looking for?" Honey asked.

"Whatever we find," Trixie said. "Was Moses brought to the doghouse by horseback? Or by someone on foot or on a motorcycle? How was he transported?"

"Now you sound like Mart," Honey teased.

"Please do not insult me like that," said Trixie haughtily.

Eventually, the girls reached the wide curve of the path opposite the intersection of Louis Road with Glen Road. Through the clearing, Trixie could see the woodsy tunnel of the little-used Louis Road on its way to the crumbling high bluffs that loomed above the Hudson River.

"Nobody could have climbed those bluffs with a baby," decided Trixie. "That means that Moses had to come from the east, north, or south."

Looking as bewildered as she felt, Honey said, "Oh, my. Where do we start looking for clues?"

"Right here!" Trixie ran down the very middle of the path.

Looking where Trixie was pointing, Honey shrugged. "Hoofprints. So what?"

"So—there were hoofprints most of the way from our gate to your stables, and here are some more. Honey, it could be the same horse. We're on the right trail!"

Honey looked thoughtful but unconvinced.

Suddenly Trixie pounced. "And here's something to prove it!" She held up a nail. Made of wrought iron, it was thin at the point, with a wedge-shaped head. It was bent from use.

"All that proves is that a nail came out of some horse's shoe," maintained Honey.

Trixie put the nail in her pocket. "Don't you see, Honey? That shoe was loose all the way from here to the rock where I found it. That's why the trail is so chopped."

"It takes six to eight nails to hold a shoe," Honey recalled. "Where are the others? And anyway, old Spartan could have thrown a shoe. So could Mr. Lytell's Belle."

"I think Spartan and Belle use larger shoes than the one I found," Trixie argued. "All these clues add up, Honey. Whoever brought Moses rode a horse! He *must* have!"

"This does place a rider in the right place at

63

the right time," admitted Honey. "But where's your horse and where's your rider? And why did you say 'he'? Usually a three-month-old baby is with his mother."

"He, she—somebody," Trixie said impatiently. She was elated to see that the hoofprints marked the trail the rest of the way to Glen Road Inn, an old Dutch mansion that had been converted into a rural hotel.

Honey looked up at the inn and fretted, "Ella might be able to see us from her window. She'll feel hurt if we don't stop in and say hi." Ella Kline was a handicapped woman who lived on the third floor. She sometimes did sewing and mending for the Wheelers.

"Let's go up," said Trixie at once. "She could have seen the horse."

"You have horse on the brain," Honey sighed.

"Oh, Honey, you know I like Ella just as much as you do," said Trixie. "I just have—you know, other things on my mind."

They found Ella in her wheelchair, beside her sewing machine. Though her brown eyes sparkled with pleasure at their visit, her hands kept on working. Her lap was heaped with the inn's linen, which she mended to earn her board and room. She was sorting articles from a huge clothes basket, then folding those that didn't require mending.

"I saw you coming," she greeted them warmly.

"We thought you might," Honey said.

While the "How are you's" and "I'm fine's" were being exchanged, Trixie walked to the window in front of Ella's sewing machine.

"Have you seen a stranger on a horse lately, Ella?" Trixie asked casually.

Honey threw her a warning frown, but Ella looked interested.

"How lately?" Ella asked.

"Like last night," Trixie said.

"My goodness, Sergeant Molinson asked me that very same question," Ella fluttered.

Trixie felt a twinge of disappointment. She'd forgotten that the sergeant had mentioned following the road all the way to the inn. And she thought she'd been so brilliant, seeking out leads from Ella.

"Why should I notice one horse?" Ella chattered on. "Seems like half the people on the Hudson own horses. Why, right over there in Chester there's a statue marking a horse's grave."

Trixie knew about Hambletonian's red granite

65

obelisk. She wasn't a really "horsey" person, but she loved the small mare, Susie, and she always listened to Regan's "horse talk." She recalled hearing that Hambletonian had fathered one thousand three hundred thirty-five foals, among them a lot of champions. If one horse reproduced himself so many times, it was impossible to imagine what New York's horse population must be. Scatter all those horses along all those roads she had thought about the previous night, and what did you have? A lot of horses and a lot of miles of roads, that's what you had.

Trixie wasn't one to become discouraged easily, but a heavy sigh escaped her. "May I use your phone, Ella?" she asked abruptly. In answer to the question in Honey's and Ella's eyes, she added, "If you don't ask questions, you won't find answers."

Still, when she had finished a stiff, short conversation with Mr. Lytell, Trixie was no closer to an answer. Swaybacked Belle, the storekeeper's aged mount, had not lost a shoe. In fact, Belle was growing fat from lack of exercise.

"We'll ask Dan about Spartan," said Honey.

"That's pointless," Trixie decided. "We both know Dan takes care of Spartan's feet. He even carries a hoof-pick in his pocket all the time."

"Whatever for?" Ella asked.

"There are lots of boggy places and rocky ridges on the game preserve," Honey explained. "Dan doesn't want Spartan's feet to become tender, so he cleans them with a hoof-pick."

"See? I'd never have known about hoof-picks if you hadn't dropped in," Ella said. Coming from another person's mouth, her words might have sounded like sarcasm, but Ella Kline was interested in the small events that made up the lives of her friends.

A voice called at the door, "It's Pete, Ella."

"Come in."

A tall teen-ager carried in a huge basket of laundry, and Ella set to work without delay. She told Trixie and Honey, "The inn has its own laundry room in the basement. It's hard for me to get to it in my wheelchair, so Pete brings a load when he has a spare minute."

Ella flipped a man's white sock into her basket.

"You didn't see if that needed mending," Trixie said.

"I mend only the inn's linen," Ella explained, "but anything that's left in a room gets washed. Someone probably kicked that sock under a bed or left it in a bathroom. Sometimes people reclaim things they leave in a room, but usually they don't. The manager gives the good stuff to charity." She held up a lace-trimmed slip. "Like this. Oh, we get all kinds of articles." She rolled her chair closer to the basket and dug to the bottom. "Some of them are kind of mysterious, too. I've been curious about this, for example. Does either of you know what it is?" She lifted up a mass of fine mesh.

Trixie shook it out, exposing dangling strong ties. "A fly sheet!" she exclaimed. Immediately, she dropped on all fours and told Honey, "Pretend I'm a horse. It's a hot day, and I'm just in from exercise. Here comes a cloud of pesky flies." Carried away by her own imagination, she whinnied with annoyance.

"Whoa, girl," coaxed Honey, getting into the spirit of the game. She draped the mesh over Trixie's back, tied the strings across her chest, and put a soft browband on her forehead. The band fell down, of course, since Trixie's head was nowhere near as large as a horse's.

"Oops, the wind must be blowing," giggled Honey. "I need a blanket pin to fasten your fly sheet under your belly."

"Watch your language," Trixie tut-tutted.

"You're the one who said you were a horse," Honey insisted.

"Don't believe everything I say," Trixie declared. "Get me out of here—this is hot! I don't see how a horse stands a sheet on a hot day."

"A horse can get a chill, even when the air is warm, if a breeze blows on his damp coat," Honey reminded her.

Ella clapped her hands as Trixie scrambled to her feet. "I always have such fun when you girls visit me! I learn about things, too."

"Useful things—like hoof-picks and fly sheets," Trixie said dryly.

"Well, if I ever find another fly sheet in my basket, at least I'll recognize it. But, Trixie, you didn't demonstrate that ropy-looking loop."

"Can't," chuckled Trixie. "That goes under the horse's tail!"

"Sorry I asked," Ella groaned, looking at the clock. "Will you girls have lunch with me?"

Trixie hesitated.

Honey, thinking that Trixie was tactlessly putting her own desire to get back on the case over Ella's feelings, cried, "We'd love to, Ella!"

Then she turned to glare at Trixie.

Sergeant Molinson Needs Help · 5

ACTUALLY, TRIXIE had paused because she'd remembered that Ella was on a small salary.

Ella seemed to sense her feeling. "It won't be fancy—just a sandwich," she went on with no embarrassment. "I'm allowed to have company as long as I don't order fresh lobster."

"Well, jeepers!" Trixie simpered, putting her finger to her cheek in a dainty gesture that would have made Mart proud. "I myself am missing green turtle soup at home today. Moms will never forgive me!"

"La-di-dah!" Honey snorted. "If I ordered that

today, our cook would send me out to catch the turtle."

"I said I was *missing* green turtle soup!" Trixie hooted. "Actually, I was going to spread peanut butter on a slab of bread."

Ella reached for the telephone. "I'm sure I can do better than that."

"I'll run down to the kitchen and pick up the order," Trixie offered.

"Pete will appreciate that. Thank you."

Trixie felt a little guilty. She wasn't trying to save steps for Pete; she wanted to see if someone in the kitchen had noticed any strange riders on the path.

When she asked the short-order cook, she received a shrewd glance. "Is something wrong up your way? Sergeant Molinson wanted to know about riders, too. The answer is no."

So he beat me to it again, thought Trixie, chagrined.

Back in Ella's room, Ella greeted Trixie with a pouting expression. "Why were you wasting time talking about horses, Trixie Belden, when you had such exciting news to tell me?" she asked.

Honey confessed that she had just told Ella about finding Moses.

"Oh . . ." Normally, Trixie didn't like to talk about a case until she had more to go on. The sergeant apparently felt the same way. Neither the cook nor Ella Kline had been questioned about a baby. The policeman had been concerned only about travelers. It just went to show that, whether beginner or professional, one could only start at the outer edge of a web and work inward, strand by strand, to find the spider.

Trixie flashed her widest grin. "I don't suppose there are baby clothes in that basket?" she hinted.

"I wish I could say yes," Ella said soberly. "Would you like to see for yourself?"

"Did the sergeant look?" Trixie asked.

Ella shook her head, and Trixie seized the chance to investigate something the sergeant had overlooked. Of course, Ella was right. There was no sign of a baby's things in her basket.

Trixie forced a smile. "Let's eat our sandwiches," she said. "All this talk about lobsters and peanut butter has got me starving!"

By the time the two girls, hot and itchy from their hours in the woods, returned to Crabapple Farm, Mrs. Belden had brought her household under control. She was enjoying the shaded backyard with Di and Moses, who lay on a well-padded blanket in a sunny spot in the grass. Di fussed to make sure the rays of the sun didn't shine directly into his eyes. She turned him on his stomach and smoothed his hair.

"How do you know when he's had enough sun?" Honey asked, plopping down near him.

"It's like ironing," replied Di. "You touch him with a damp finger. If he sizzles, he's had enough." Di kept a perfectly straight face except for her pansy-colored eyes, which sparkled with mischief.

"Come on," Honey begged. "Remember, I was an only child most of my life. Jim was fifteen years old when he joined the family!"

Di turned serious. "We're watching the clock over there on the steps and keeping close track of his skin color."

Trixie touched the baby's roughened, chapped skin. "Whoever had him last wasn't so careful," she said softly.

"I'm a better sitter than that whoever," Di declared.

Di went home to dinner in the late afternoon, and soon it was time for Trixie and Honey to share the baby's six o'clock feeding. The two girls arrived at the Belden dinner table radiant with renewed energy.

"Are you just ego-tripping in general?" inquired Mart. "Or did the baby succumb to your indoctrination and tell you he wants to be a detective when he grows up?"

Trixie glared at him, but Honey had to giggle. "Neither," she told him. "There's just—oh, you know, something special about a baby."

"Your point is well taken," Mart agreed. "I'd recite a poem for you concerning youth's incorruptibility, but, alas, I myself am too old to remember such innocence."

"Oh, Mart," sighed his mother, "if you talk this way at fifteen, you're going to be an unbearable old man." Before Mart had a chance to defend himself, she turned to Mr. Belden. "Peter, I do wish you'd look at our washing machine. Something seems to have caught in the spinning basket."

Mr. Belden waggled dark brows at his family. "I'm sure someone else could handle it better."

"I'll take care of it," said Brian, who was used to tinkering with his jalopy.

Jim arrived as the group was finishing dinner, and he rumpled Honey's hair when he passed

74

her chair. "Who's the new boarder?" he queried. "She vaguely resembles a sister I used to have."

Honey wrinkled her nose. "Seems to me that when I last saw you, dear brother, you were in this very house, too."

"And here I plan to stay," said Jim. "I volunteer for the ten o'clock feeding. But—" he paused dramatically—"I do not come empty-handed. Miss Trask sent a freezer of black walnut ice cream and a coconut cake as partial payment on our board bill."

Mart jumped up to offer Jim his chair. "Why didn't you say so?" he whooped. Serving dishes had only just been emptied of baked ham, garden vegetables, and scalloped potatoes, but Mart was always ready to eat.

"Hollow legs," muttered his father.

"Toes, too," Bobby said.

Minutes later, Dan Mangan rode Spartan down the bridle trail. Trixie came out to greet him, and even while she was saying hello, she was looking at Spartan's great hooves. Almost covered by long, white feathering hairs, his feet were well cared for. No shoes were missing, and, as Trixie had suspected, Spartan also wore a much larger shoe than the one she had found.

"It's time I saw that baby," Dan demanded.

"You'll love him," said Trixie as she led Dan to the clothes basket.

Too listless to play, Moses still was able to turn his head and follow a source of sound with alert eyes. Dan stood beside him for several minutes before touching one tiny hand. Fingers moved, found Dan's thumb, and clung. Dan was so thrilled that he refused to take his hand away until Moses went to sleep.

While standing with Dan near Moses' basket, Trixie noticed that the hooked rug by the guest-room beds seemed a little crooked. When she went to straighten it, she found a few clods of dried mud on the rug. Trixie frowned. Grandma Belden had made that rug when she was young. She had designed it, dyed the wool, and spent countless hours pulling yarn through canvas. Beldens were under strict orders to keep muddy feet off of it. Trixie collected the clods, then went to answer the doorbell.

Di stood on the porch steps, and Trixie could see the Lynch Cadillac in the driveway.

"Someone has to take me home, or else I'll have to stay all night," announced Di in her usual polite tones.

"Stay," Trixie invited. "You can share the two o'clock feeding."

At once, Di turned around and yelled, "See you in the morning, Dad!"

Trixie and Di were soon joined on the porch by the rest of the Beldens and Bob-Whites. While Jim scooped out masses of cold creamy goodness, Honey cut and served the coconut cake. Doves called from their high perches, and swallows swooped for insects just above the tops of maples and oaks.

Bobby divided his time between eating his treat and chasing lightning bugs. When his mesh-covered jar contained three miniature flashlights, he wanted to go in and share them with Moses.

"Don't you dare," Trixie warned. "If you wake him up, I'll put him in your room for you to take care of."

"Neato!" Bobby chirped.

"When are we going to have Mo's party?" bubbled Di.

"We're having one now," Jim said.

"No, a *real* party, with a long dress for him, and—"

"Dress!" Bobby hooted. "Moses is a boy!"

77

"You wore a dress when you got your name," Mart informed him.

"I did not!" Bobby roared.

"Get the photograph album," Mrs. Belden said, "and see for yourself."

Bobby huffed into the house and came back with the family album, which he examined using a flashlight. Baby pictures were mounted on the first page, one child dark like Mr. Belden and three children as fair as Mrs. Belden.

"Everybody's got dresses on," Bobby groaned in disbelief, "even Brian." With great dignity, he closed the album.

"Babies wear dresses to dress up," Di explained. "Let's have the party at my house Sunday. That will give me plenty of time to find one of the twins' dresses and plan the treats."

"What shall we bring?" Trixie asked.

"Just Moses Bob-White," Di said happily.

Down at the end of the lane, headlights loomed out of the darkness and moved toward the house.

"Oh, no," Di moaned, "Mother's sent Harrison after me."

Instead of the Lynch butler, it was Sergeant Molinson who stepped out of the car and came to the porch steps.

78

"Would you like some ice cream, sir?" Jim asked politely.

To Trixie's surprise, the sergeant accepted Jim's offer gratefully. Usually he had such an attitude of gruff authority that it was hard to imagine him doing something as human as slurping ice cream. As he ate, he stretched his long legs and, with his free hand, rubbed his lower back.

"Tired?" Peter Belden asked.

"It's been a long day," Sergeant Molinson admitted. "I've been checking out every possible lead on the baby—in between stopping bar fights and investigating robberies and dealing with assorted drifters and drunks. This August heat is getting on everyone's nerves. The crime rate always seems to rise around this time of year."

Trixie thought that the sergeant looked like a person with several problems too many. Maybe . . .

Trixie gulped, shocked at the idea that had just occurred to her. Maybe the sergeant would accept help on this case from the Belden-Wheeler Detective Agency! Any other day, it was like pulling teeth to get him to admit that Trixie Belden and Honey Wheeler made his work easier. *But tonight* . . .

Prudently, Trixie began to arrange her arguments in her mind before presenting them to the officer. Now: The farm was the scene of the crime. . . .

"Trixie!"

With glazed eyes, Trixie searched for the speaker.

"Trixie, the sergeant has spoken to you twice," said Mr. Belden.

"I'm sorry," Trixie said hastily. "I—I guess I was thinking."

"Eating ice cream and thinking at the same time has been a difficult act for my sister to add to her repertoire," Mart explained. "Such coordination can't be picked up overnight, you know."

Trixie resisted the urge to punch Mart and turned to the officer. "Yes, sir?"

"I was wondering if you could give me a hand on this baby case tonight."

"Wh-What?" Trixie stammered. Was it possible that he was actually asking for her help at the exact moment when she was prepared to volunteer it?

"I'm including Miss Wheeler, of course," the sergeant went on.

"W-We'd be . . ." Trixie began.

". . . glad to!" Honey finished eagerly.

"I thought so," said the sergeant. "Now, where's the baby?"

"He's asleep," Mrs. Belden said. "I'm afraid he—"

"I won't bother him any more than I have to," promised the sergeant. "First, let's take a look at this picture of two missing boys." He took a picture from his hip pocket. "See if you recognize the baby." He passed the photo to Trixie first.

Brian got up and turned on the porch light. Blinking rapidly to adjust her eyes to the light change, Trixie stared at the picture of the two boys, one somewhat older than Bobby, the other an infant younger than Moses. The baby was bald. His eyes were fixed on a rattle the older boy held before his face.

"I can't tell," Trixie admitted at last.

"Here, let me look at that!" scoffed Mart. After a long moment, he, too, said sheepishly that he wasn't sure.

Even Brian, who looked at bone construction, could not swear that the baby was Moses.

"Babies change from day to day, sometimes

from hour to hour," Mrs. Belden said as she handed the picture back to the sergeant. "One day we say he's just the picture of his father, and the next day we see only the slightest resemblance."

"I guess I'd better take a look at the baby in person," the sergeant decided.

Trixie escorted him to the guest room. At the door, she flicked on a lamp and waited to see if Moses mewed before she crossed the room. She beckoned the sergeant to follow her. In that brief instant, it seemed to her that the hooked rug was out of place again.

With photograph in hand, the sergeant stood beside the clothes basket and stared down at Moses. Trixie, too, looked from Moses to the picture and back again many times. After only twenty-four hours of careful attention, Moses was losing the neglected, battered look that had caused so much concern. Pinkly clean, he smelled of talcum and baby oil. One tiny fist was raised above his ear, his thumb folded across his cupped palm.

Trixie felt like putting her finger in that hand, to feel the warmth and total dependence of his small body. Instead, she followed the sergeant as

82

he awkwardly tiptoed from the room. Once the two were back out on the porch, the sergeant took command.

"I still don't know if that's the same kid," he told the group, "but among all of the Missing Persons reports and photos, only the baby in this picture seems to fill the bill. The problem is, there are two kids missing, Davy and Robert. You may have found Robert." He paused and scratched his head. "It'll be a shock to the parents if I call them to identify Robert and can't produce Davy."

"Won't it be a worse shock if you call them to come here and Moses isn't Robert after all?" Honey spoke up quietly.

The sergeant agreed, and Trixie quickly followed her friend's lead. "Why don't we just take the baby right to the parents?" she suggested. "If we suddenly appear at their door with a baby, they won't have had time to build false hopes, in case Moses is someone else's son."

"I was hoping you'd think of that," the sergeant said. "It's already occurred to me that you two girls might go along with me to the Dodges' house. You could watch the baby while I'm driving and also give a firsthand report to the

83

parents on how he was found."

Something clicked in Trixie's brain. "The Dodges—you mean the family over on Saw Mill River?"

The sergeant nodded.

"Oh, Peter," Mrs. Belden put in worriedly. "Isn't that the man you were talking about—the one whose belongings were auctioned because he couldn't get a loan?"

"Apparently it is," said Peter Belden, frowning.

"That's too much trouble to have all at the same time!" Trixie cried. She scrambled to her feet. "I'll go get Moses. I certainly hope he turns out to be Robert Dodge."

"They'll still have trouble," Bobby declared suddenly. " 'Cause where's Davy?"

All eyes peered into the dark that had thickened to the texture of rich velvet. Yes, where *was* Davy?

Kidnapped? • 6

INSIDE THE POLICE CAR, Trixie held Moses on her lap while Honey looked after the supplies they would need for his ten-o'clock feeding. To relieve the tension they all were feeling, Trixie spoke in a droning, soft voice of the clues she and Honey had uncovered in the woods. "There's even a horse's fly sheet in Ella Kline's laundry basket," she finished.

"What's that got to do with anything?" the sergeant grunted.

"I'm just telling you what we found," Trixie replied. She became aware that they had entered the "spider web," the tangle of roads that included Taconic State Parkway, Saw Mill River Parkway, Saw Mill River Road, and all the other roads and highways. The Dodge property was somewhere in this confusing jumble.

The sergeant soon turned onto a private road. The police car's headlights illuminated boulders, a brook, and trees. Except for the road and the electric wires that threaded through trees and flashed slivers of silver when touched by light, the strip of land seemed untouched by civilization. The car came to a halt in a driveway.

Trixie carefully hoisted Moses against her shoulder and allowed the sergeant to help her from the car. Honey followed with the supplies.

At the end of the driveway, a yard light blackened the shadows around an old, yellow brick farmhouse with a steeply pitched gable roof. Lonely silence seemed to flow like a current around the closely clustered buildings that made up the farmstead. No horse bumped a stall with his hoof. No cow muttered in her sleep. No hen scolded. There wasn't even a dog to bark.

Recalling that the Dodges had held an auction, Trixie asked anxiously, "Are you sure the people still live here?"

"This is where I picked up the photograph this morning," the sergeant said. He led the way and hammered at the blue wooden door. When there was no answer, he lifted the antique knocker, a gargoyle's head, to hammer again.

At last, the door opened a crack, and a man asked, "Who's there?" It was a young voice, strained and tense.

The sergeant held out his identification.

"Oh, yes, Sergeant Molinson," the man said.

Trixie followed directly behind the policeman as they entered the Dodge house. She saw a young man in his mid-thirties, with electric blue eyes and stylishly cut brown hair.

"Come in," he said. "Here, let me move that box so you can sit down. As you can see, we're pretty much in a mess around here. We're packing and—" Suddenly he stopped his restless speech and said, "Do you have news about our boys?" His eyes blazed with intense emotion.

The sergeant stepped aside to bring Trixie and her bundle to the young man's attention. "We've brought a child," he began.

In two long strides, David Dodge crossed the cluttered room. He moved the thin blanket to uncover Moses' face. Work-hardened farmer's fingers, well scrubbed but stained, shook so much that the blanket fluttered when he touched it.

Trixie became uncomfortably aware of the thump of her own heart as seconds seemed to stretch into an eternity. Warmth from Moses' body seemed to spread to her arms and creep through her veins and arteries all the way to her toes, while she watched those electric blue eyes, shaded by a tangle of curly lashes, widen and close, widen and close.

"Are you all right, Mr. Dodge?" Honey asked nervously. She put out a hand and touched his elbow. "Are you going to faint?"

"No!" Without touching the baby, he swung around and bellowed, "Eileen! Come here! Dodgy is home! *Dodgy is home!*"

Trixie heard a thin cry from someone on the second floor, then a rush of feet. The last five steps of the narrow stairway were not boxed in. Trixie started to yell as she saw a bare foot reach for that first exposed riser and miss the step. With incredible speed, David Dodge leaped over a packing box and prevented his wife's fall. The two came forward, clinging to and supporting each other. Both were crying and making no effort to stop the tears.

"It's Dodgy, honey—he's home!" the man said.

Mrs. Dodge was almost as tall as her husband but slightly built and blond. Her eyes were large and blue, the lids puffed by tears. She wore tailored cotton pajamas and no slippers.

For an instant, Trixie was chilled with fear. What if David Dodge's apparent state of shock had persuaded him that this was his child . . . when it was not?

But it was. Oh, it was.

The minute Trixie placed the baby in Eileen Dodge's arms, she felt the change of temperature of her own skin. Shivering, she folded her arms and backed against Honey. Together the girls watched the young parents examine and wonder and murmur. All the while, their tears of relief flowed unchecked down their shining faces.

The child they called Dodgy stirred, wakened, looked with wide, unwinking dark eyes, and grabbed handfuls of air. Eileen Dodge laid her cheek against his, and his tiny hand latched onto her blond hair. He obviously recognized the security of her touch and began to mew like a kitten. Someplace in the house, a clock chimed.

"Ten o'clock," Honey said. "I have his supplies. Would you like me to heat his formula so

89

you can feed him, Mrs. Dodge?" And she moved toward the kitchen visible through a doorway.

"Feed him?" the young mother repeated. Then she sparkled, "Oh, yes!" Suddenly she took notice of the strangers in her home. She said, "Sit down, won't you? Who . . . ? I mean, I'm Eileen Dodge, and this is my husband, David, and this is my son, Robert, and . . ."

She stopped her rushing words and cried, "Where's Davy?" She held her baby so closely that Trixie could see the knotted muscles in her arms. Her voice dropped to a hoarse whisper. *"Where is Davy?"*

For the second time that night, Trixie saw a side of the hardheaded policeman she hadn't known existed. He stepped forward to pat the woman's shoulders, as if he were comforting a child. "Ssh, ssh, Mrs. Dodge. Ssh, ssh." In a short while, the sergeant's calm voice had soothed the mother, and he said, "Now, listen to me while I explain what's happened."

Eileen Dodge drew in her breath and stopped crying, but she did not loosen her hold on the baby. Automatically, she took the warm bottle Honey brought from the kitchen and began his feeding.

"These are my young, uh, friends, Trixie Belden and Honey Wheeler. They both live a couple of miles from Sleepyside, on Glen Road. Your baby was abandoned at Trixie's house during Wednesday's storm. As I understand it, your children disappeared Saturday. Is that right?"

"About noon Saturday," David Dodge said.

The sergeant nodded. "We haven't figured out yet where they were in that period between Saturday noon and Wednesday night. We still don't know where Davy is . . . but, well, here's Robert, all safe and sound. Now we can direct all our efforts toward finding Davy."

The Dodge couple's reaction to this explanation was bewildering, to say the least.

Eileen cried, "No!" and hugged the baby so tightly that he squeaked.

David patted his wife's back with one hand and rubbed his own head with the other, evidently trying to make up his mind about something. Didn't they *want* Davy?

The sergeant frowned at the odd behavior. "What's going on here?" he demanded harshly.

"Look—" David Dodge began.

"No!" his wife interrupted. "David, the note says don't call the police!"

91

"I know, but . . ."

"What note?" the sergeant barked.

"No!" Eileen cried again.

"I have to tell him, honey," David pleaded. "It's our only chance to get Davy back!" He left the room abruptly and returned with two sheets of paper. He gave one to the sergeant and explained, "As you can see, this one is from Davy."

Sergeant Molinson held the paper in such a way that Trixie and Honey could read along with him.

"Dere Mom and Dad," said the note, "I am running away and I am not never coming back. I won't let you sell"—at this point, he had tried to spell Dodgy and had apparently given up—"D. and me. I luv you, Davy."

"What does he mean, sell?" Sergeant Molinson inquired.

"I wish I knew," David answered wearily. "That's been giving me nightmares. We didn't find the note till after the auction. We've been out of our minds with worry. We've searched, night and day, but things have been so up for grabs around here that—well, we wouldn't recognize a clue if it jumped up and bit us."

The fact that the sergeant was treating her

as an equal gave Trixie the courage to say, "I should think you'd have noticed the baby was gone. Who was taking care of him?"

Eileen moaned. "Please don't blame me. I can't stand any more! I blame myself. I can't sleep, I can't eat. . . ." She rocked with Dodgy and started crying again.

David rubbed the back of his wife's tense neck while he answered Trixie's question. "Eileen had given Dodgy his morning feeding. A neighbor girl was supposed to watch him while he took his nap in the shade of the house, out of the way of the auction traffic. She didn't report a problem, so Eileen went right ahead showing furniture and stuff inside the house while the auctioneers worked in the barn. She didn't notice how late it was getting. Besides, the girl often gave Dodgy his bottle. We trusted her." David's voice broke.

"What was her story?" the sergeant asked, his face expressionless.

"She had a boyfriend who was in the crowd. She wanted to let him know she was here. She said she was gone 'just a minute,' but when she came back, Dodgy was gone. She figured Eileen had taken him into the house, so she felt free to join the crowd. She thought somebody would call her if she was needed. Nobody did, so she went home."

"Didn't anybody pay her?" Honey asked alertly.

"Eileen had told her we'd pay her after the auction money was in." David looked embarrassed, and Trixie recalled what her father had said about this man's carelessness with money. "We—we owed her for several sittings and were going to pay her at the end of the month. She—she was a good baby-sitter; I'm sure she doesn't have anything to do with the kidnapping."

"Are you sure the note is from Davy?" Sergeant Molinson asked.

"Yes," David said.

"Then *why* do you suspect kidnapping?" the sergeant snapped.

"We didn't, until—" David opened the second note and stared at it, apparently unwilling to share it.

Then he changed his mind and shoved the note into the sergeant's hand. "We found this under the door Sunday morning. That's why we were late in turning in a picture of the boys. We didn't want to risk their lives. But there's a limit to how much a person can stand. We've got to have help!"

Again Trixie and Honey read the note along with Sergeant Molinson.

" 'We have your boys,' " Trixie read aloud. " 'Don't call the police if you ever expect to see them again. We'll bargain with you later, when you've had time to think about this.' "

"What they mean," said David bitterly, "is when we've had time to drive ourselves crazy, so that we'll meet any terms they suggest."

By this time, Eileen had finished feeding the baby and was raising him to her shoulder. Trixie could hear the soft patting of her hands. Eileen had pretty hands, gentle and capable. She couldn't have inflicted those bruises on that baby's helpless body.

"Which note did you find first?" Trixie asked.

Sergeant Molinson quirked an approving eyebrow at her.

"Davy's," answered Eileen. "It was pinned to the pillow in Dodgy's bed. We found it Saturday afternoon. That's when we found the broken piggy banks and discovered that some formula bottles were missing."

The sergeant waved Davy's note. "You don't

95

think he was forced to write the note?"

"No," David said firmly. "I honestly think he took Dodgy and ran away for some mixed-up reason of his own. What happened to him after that is anybody's guess."

"You haven't found another note?"

"No, so we've been hoping that the second one was some kind of cruel prank. But—" David shrugged helplessly— "none of our neighbors are the kind who would do a thing like that."

The sergeant paced about the room, evidently thinking deeply. The Dodges, Trixie, and Honey watched him silently. The baby slept on his mother's lap. Trixie could hear the ticktock of that upstairs clock.

Eileen smiled slightly, noticing that Trixie was listening to the clock. "We didn't sell the clock," she said. "It's been in our family for generations, and Davy likes it. He says it puts him to sleep at night and keeps him company if he happens to wake up."

Trixie tried to return Eileen's smile, but it died before it reached her lips. Where was Davy tonight? No place where an antique clock chimed, she could bet on that.

David looked at Trixie. "Tell us about Dodgy."

Again Trixie repeated the story of the discovery of the baby in the doghouse, and of the care he had received since then. "He has bruises we can't account for," she said.

"Bruises!" Hastily Eileen Dodge lifted the gown to examine the tiny body. The sounds she made showed both her outrage and her deep concern. "I don't understand this. Dodgy has never even had a rash!"

"Were there any clues to show how he got to the doghouse?" David asked.

"I found a horseshoe nearby," Trixie told him.

"Could D. D. have ridden Wicky?" Eileen asked her husband.

"D. D.?" Honey repeated.

"That's Davy. We're such a nicknaming family," Eileen explained. "D. D. is for David Dodge, Junior. Dodgy is for Robert, because we started out calling him the new Dodge. D. D. had a pony named Wicky, short for Wickcliff. I thought Wicky was sold at the auction, but D. D. might have got his hands on him first."

"Putting a baby in a doghouse sounds like something a child Davy's age might do," David Dodge mused.

"I agree with you," Sergeant Molinson said, stopping his pacing to stand beside Trixie's chair. "But how does that fit in with the second note?"

"I think—" Both Trixie and Honey began to speak at the same time.

Trixie often spoke from impulse, while Honey was more apt to reason. With Sergeant Molinson actually allowing them to work with him, even just for the evening, they really ought to make the best impression. "You go first," urged Trixie.

Honey's pretty face flushed with earnestness. "I think, for the safety of both children, we can't ignore the possibility that the note is genuine. I—I don't know why a ransom note would be sent after Davy had run away, but it does tell me that someone is watching this house. Somebody knows the boys are missing and—"

"—and that person wants to take advantage of it. Is that what you're saying?" the sergeant asked sharply.

Honey's skin was not as thick as Trixie's. It obviously rattled her to be spoken to in that tone of voice, but she stood her ground bravely. "Yes, sir. I'm wondering what will happen to Davy when they discover that the baby has been found and returned home."

"And," Trixie added quickly, "what if they decide to snatch Dodgy when they see he's back here?"

"What'll we do?" Eileen Dodge gasped. Frantically her eyes darted from the baby to her husband, then to the sergeant, Trixie, and Honey.

Again the sergeant paced, and again Trixie could hear the clock, as well as the hum of the refrigerator and a sound that might have been an electric fan in a bedroom. Trixie had the kind of mind that was receptive to what her five senses told her, and she had the ability to place bits and pieces of information into mental pigeonholes for further reference. Mart said she would never be a poet, but who cared? She was going to be a full-fledged detective one day! Now that she was technically doing police work, that day seemed to move into some middle ground between the future and the present.

"We could take the baby back home with us," Trixie suggested finally.

The sergeant looked skeptical, then glanced at his wristwatch. The strain of his long day was beginning to show on his face. "I can't think of a better solution at the moment. I think we've done all we can do tonight. Is that plan all right with you, Mr. and Mrs. Dodge?"

"I won't let him go!" Eileen Dodge declared. Tears seemed imminent.

Hesitantly Honey spoke up. "Sergeant, would it be all right if Mrs. Dodge came with us, to help take care of Dodgy until the case is solved?"

Eileen brightened. "I like that idea," she admitted shyly.

"The kidnappers, if they're watching the house, won't notice she and the baby are gone," Honey said, "if they leave with us tonight, in the dark."

"Well," Sergeant Molinson put in, "we'll just have to take that chance, anyway. They may not be watching the house all that closely."

"And," Trixie chimed in, "she would be right on the spot to help Honey and me with any clues we turn up in searching for Davy."

"You're going to search for clues." The sergeant did not ask a question; he made a statement of fact.

"You asked Honey and me to work on this case, remember?" Trixie said hopefully.

"I meant help me deliver the baby to his parents tonight," the man said stiffly.

100

Unexpectedly, David Dodge came to the girls' rescue. "Sergeant, it seems to me that Trixie and Honey could be very helpful. They've done so much for us already, and they're obviously alert and intelligent. Besides, it'll throw these kidnappers off the trail. It won't occur to them that a couple of teen-agers are actually working hand in hand with the police department."

"You have a point," decided the sergeant. "All right—Trixie and Honey, you may keep your eyes peeled for clues as to the whereabouts of Davy. However, under no circumstances are you allowed to search for the kidnappers, and we must assume that some type of kidnappers are involved here. Leave them to the police, you understand?"

Trixie's head was spinning from David's compliments and the sergeant's agreement, but Honey managed to stammer, "Y-Yes, sir!"

David looked relieved and turned to his wife. "You keep in touch, now, dear, okay?"

She bobbed her head up and down. "Just a minute, I'll get changed and pack some clothes!" This time Eileen Dodge did not miss a step when she used the stairway.

The Missing Horseshoe · 7

ONLY BOBBY HAD GONE to bed by the time the group reached Crabapple Farm. Di, Mart, Jim, Dan, and Brian were arguing amiably over a Monopoly game, while the senior Beldens were watching the news on television.

Mart looked up when he heard the footsteps on the porch and yelped, "It's about time you got back!"

Di jumped up and ran to the screen door. "Were they Moses' parents?" Seeing the baby without noticing who carried him, she cried, "Oh, I'm sorry!"

"Don't be sorry!" Trixie lilted. "Dodgy likes his room so much that he brought his mother back to share it with him!"

"Dodgy? Who's Dodgy?" Brian wanted to know.

"Robert! Moses! Brian, his name—I mean, his nickname—is Dodgy," Honey replied.

The two groups met and mingled, those who had stayed home and those who had traveled. Everybody talked at once. Hands reached to touch Dodgy; hands reached to shake Eileen Dodge's hand. Mart got so carried away he even shook hands with the sergeant. "Great job, sir!" he said.

"Well, thanks, Mart," Sergeant Molinson said. "It's time I got back to the station." As he turned to head toward his car, he looked at Trixie and Honey and warned, "Keep me posted."

Once Eileen had put Dodgy to bed, she joined Trixie and Honey in the telling of the Dodge story. At one point, she flushed and said, "I hope I won't inconvenience you, Mrs. Belden. I just realized that I've invited myself to your home."

"No, Mrs. Dodge," Honey interrupted, "I was the one who invited you, so really I should insist on taking you home to Manor House."

"Call me Eileen," Mrs. Dodge urged.

"Thank you, Honey," Mrs. Belden said, "but I'm sure we can make Eileen and Dodgy comfortable here. Now that Dodgy has been found, I'm sure it won't be long until Davy is back, safe and sound."

By the time the lights were turned out at Crabapple Farm and Trixie was in her own bed, with Di sleeping in the matching twin bed, she knew just how the sergeant felt. It had been a long, hard day. She, too, was tired, yet still so wound up that sleep would not come to her immediately.

She recalled the hopelessness she had felt twenty-four hours before, when she had realized that finding the baby's parents would involve sifting multitudes of people through a screen. One day later, because of the love and concern of total strangers, that baby had a name and a mother to guard him. And, wonder of wonders, she and Honey were to work with the sergeant in the all-out search for the baby's brother.

Trixie's mind gnawed impatiently at the problem. Because of the total upset at the Dodge farm, it would be difficult to conduct the search from that end of Davy's trail. Anyway, she didn't fool herself into thinking that she could walk in and find clues that Davy's own parents had missed.

Logically, therefore, she must begin her search right here at the farm. So far, all indications were that whoever had left Dodgy in the doghouse had ridden a horse. Well, Davy had owned a pony. His parents weren't sure if Wicky had been auctioned, but surely that could be checked. Yawning, Trixie decided that her first step was to ask her father how an auction was conducted. He'd know.

Just on the verge of sleep, Trixie roused herself to whisper, "Regan!" Regan would know if that horseshoe she'd found matched whatever Davy's pony turned out to be. Of course, kidnappers could be holding both the boy and his horse, but Trixie refused to let herself dwell on that possibility.

She felt goose bumps rise on her skin as she recalled placing Dodgy in his mother's arms. Jeepers, if only she could do the same for his brother. *Oh, happy day. . . .*

She had to work carefully. A criminal might just be waiting for someone to make a mistake. Trixie sighed heavily, aware of the burden of responsibility she bore. As she dozed off, she heard Reddy bark once. *Poor dog,* she thought. *He still hasn't recovered from the invasion of his property.* . . .

The following morning, as Trixie and Di got dressed, Di bubbled with excitement. She had waked at two o'clock to help Eileen with Dodgy's care. "She didn't know her way around your kitchen, but I did," Di said. Anxiously she added, "Do you suppose she managed the six o'clock feeding by herself?"

"She's the baby's mother, silly. After all, she's used to running a farmhouse while taking care of two children and a husband."

"True," Di agreed. "But that was in her house, not this one."

"What's the matter with this house?" Trixie retorted. "Moms has raised four kids here!"

"I love your house," Di began earnestly.

"Oh, I'm sorry for snapping at you," said Trixie. "I guess I didn't get enough sleep."

"I found some nickels and dimes on the kitchen table," said Di as the two girls went downstairs. "I put them on the refrigerator and closed the refrigerator door. It was open when I went to the kitchen."

"Open?" Trixie repeated. "Moms'll scalp Mart. He's always so careless about that door."

"Oh, I hope she doesn't," Di giggled. "I like Mart's scalp!"

Trixie rushed into the kitchen, saying, "Dad, I need to talk to you—" She stopped in consternation. His chair was empty. She turned to her mother, who was expertly scrambling eggs. "Hasn't Dad come down yet? He'll be late to work."

"Money. Filthy lucre—that's all you think about," Mart mourned between bites of bacon.

"Your father had a Chamber of Commerce breakfast to attend this morning," said Mrs. Belden.

"But I—" Trixie gulped down her disappointment. Oh, well. She could still consult Regan this morning.

Soon Eileen Dodge entered the kitchen. Amid the chorus of "Good morning's," she took the place at the table that Brian offered.

Trixie noticed that the puffiness was gone from around Eileen's blue eyes, but her face was still so drawn that the skin seemed to be too tight for even her fine bones.

"I am grateful for your hospitality," Eileen

said somewhat formally, "but I'm not sure I should be here. What if David hears—" she hesitated— "b-bad news about D. D.? He'll need me. And if our house is being watched, they're bound to notice I'm not there."

Mrs. Belden arranged an attractive plate of food and passed it to Eileen. "Why don't you at least stay long enough to meet Dr. Ferris?" she suggested. "He's coming out this morning to examine the baby. It will put your mind at ease to hear his report firsthand."

"Oh, yes," Eileen agreed. "I have to find out what caused those bruises and how to heal them."

"We've been treating them," Brian told her. "That was approved by Miss Goodley, the social worker from the county welfare department."

"W-Welfare?" Eileen stammered. "Just as soon as we settle up with the auctioneers—"

"This isn't a matter of inability to pay bills," Mrs. Belden explained gently. "Abandoned children are the state's responsibility. The police delegated Dodgy to our care during the investigation. I do feel you should let us help you. Forgive me for saying so, but I don't think you're in shape emotionally or physically to cope with

Dodgy's total care until your older son is found."

Eileen's hand shook as she lifted her coffee cup. "I—I have been so worried and scared that I was afraid I was losing my mind," she admitted quietly.

"You're among friends, Eileen," Brian said.

"I am grateful," Eileen repeated.

Trixie took a deep breath and glanced through her lashes at Di. Di, too, was so moved by Eileen's confusion that she was having trouble swallowing her food. Trixie forced herself to finish her meal, her heart aching for Eileen.

"Does somebody have time to look at the washer?" Mrs. Belden asked hopefully.

Brian had already left the kitchen, and Mart was preparing to follow. He heaped buttered toast with jam to take with him. "Later, Moms," he promised. "My elder counterpart doth crack a mighty whip. I wouldst away before I incur his displeasure."

"Brian isn't working in the woods," grunted Bobby. "I heard Dad tell him to irri-something the raspberries this morning."

"Irritate?" Mart guessed on his way out the door.

Bobby looked doubtful.

"Irrigate," Trixie told Bobby. "Gleeps, with Mart for a teacher, Bobby'll never learn to speak English!"

Eyes sparkling, Di put in, "But, Trixie, Mart is so smart!"

"How nice to have your very own fan club," muttered Trixie as she began to clear the breakfast table.

"I'll help," Di offered.

They had just finished the kitchen work when Harrison, the Lynch butler, came for Di. She rushed to check up on Dodgy before climbing into the limousine. "If you need me, just call," she urged.

"Thanks, Di," Trixie answered. She returned to her morning work with a mind churning with plans. She had been fumbling around, trying to get a grip on the mystery. She had found it, but where to now?

The minute her morning chores were finished, Trixie called Honey. "Meet me at the stables?"

"Are we going to ride?" Honey asked. "What shall I wear?"

"Just wear what you have on now."

"A bath towel? I just took a shower!"

Trixie giggled. "You're out of uniform, Detective Wheeler. Let's wear shorts and wait to ride till it's cooler, okay? I'll be there in fifteen minutes."

When Trixie reached the stables, she heard Honey call, "Trix, I'm in the supply room. There's a fan here."

Trixie called back, "I'm stopping at the tack room first." She went straight to the shelf where she had thrown the horseshoe. She patted the entire length of the shelf, then patted again.

"Honey, it's gone," she wailed. "The horseshoe's gone!"

Honey hurried down the wide alleyway. "Regan probably threw it in the scrap heap. There's a bin behind the barn."

As Trixie rushed after Honey to the barn, she breathed in the familiar odors of timothy, clover, bran, oats, leather, saddle soap, and horseflesh. Everything was in order. She should have known Regan would notice that shoe.

The scrap bin was a huge wooden box with a hinged lid held in place by a hasp. It took the girls' combined strength to lift the lid. Trixie stared in dismay at the bits of chain, the bars of metal and tools without handles, the odds-and-ends leftovers from Regan's world.

"Where do we start?" Trixie asked.

"At the top," Honey said practically. "Help me lift this wheelbarrow frame. There's small stuff under it."

"How'd you recognize a wheelbarrow frame?" Trixie asked in amazement.

Honey grinned. "I saw the gardener take the barrow apart."

With the first plunge into the scrap, both girls broke fingernails and got rust smeared on skin and clothing.

"And you've just had a shower," Trixie said apologetically.

"We have lots of soap," Honey retorted cheerfully. "Just tell me why we're doing this."

"If we find that shoe," Trixie explained, "we can use it to check tracks we run across and locate that horse. Davy may be on that horse. And Regan can identify that shoe for us."

As if on cue, just then Regan came around the corner of the barn. Hooking both thumbs in his wide belt, he queried, "Going into the junk business?"

"The horseshoe, Regan!" Trixie cried. "Where is it?"

For a second, Regan blanked. Then he asked,

"You mean that Shetland shoe Dan found on a shelf?"

"Shetland?" Although Trixie had guessed that the horse was smaller than Spartan, it wasn't until her visit to the Dodges that it occurred to her that the lost shoe might have belonged to a pony. Even so, she dared not raise her hopes too high. Bobby had recently learned to ride while Regan had trained a Shetland named Mr. Pony. Mr. Pony could have lost that shoe on the bicycle trail. That was one of the few trails Bobby had been allowed to use.

Regan didn't have to be told that Trixie had put the shoe on the shelf. Her drooping lips and shoulders were tattlers. "Where'd you find it, Trix?"

Trixie told him.

The tall, red-haired groom nodded. "Molinson's already been here looking for a transient horse. None of our horses had lost shoes. There was this extra shoe, so we gave it to him."

Trixie thrust her sneaker toe against the scrap bin and tried to think of a way of dealing with this discouraging development. She had counted on finding that shoe.

Wet Soap and a Tepee · 8

Regan said kindly, "If it will make you feel better, Trix, Molinson told me you were the one who put him on the trail of the horse."

Trixie tried smiling but failed. "Let's go take a bath while we think of a new plan, Honey."

"You going to give up, just like that?"

Alertly Trixie turned on Regan. "Why? Do you know something else?"

"I might."

"Tell us!" Trixie begged. "This case is awfully important to Honey and me. Yipes, Sergeant Molinson has actually asked us for help, and we don't want to blow it. We simply have to find that missing boy."

"Boy?" Regan repeated. "Thought we were talking about a horse."

Honey filled Regan in on the story of Davy.

"Well," Regan mused, "after Molinson left, I got to thinking about that shoe and wondering why it was so important to find a transient horse. You know, you can tell a lot about people by the way they take care of their horses."

Trixie's eyes swept the wide, peaceful scene. Clean, fly-free stables, a supply barn that allowed for the circulation of fresh air, whitewashed fences, and meadow corners without weeds—all these things reflected Regan's love of animals, and Matthew Wheeler's good sense in hiring Regan.

"I knew that was no keg shoe," Regan went on.

"What's that?" Trixie wanted to know.

"A factory-made iron plate ordered by blacksmiths in bulk in kegs. An ordinary riding hack can use them with no trouble if he doesn't have foot problems. Now, a race animal would have been wearing aluminum plates so thin they'd only be good for one race."

"The shoe wasn't that thin," Trixie said.

"I agree," Regan said. "And it didn't belong to a walking horse. They sometimes carry into the show ring as much as thirty-six ounces on each foot."

Trixie shook her head. "It wasn't that heavy."

"There you go," Regan said. "It was simply a matter of elimination, shoe by shoe, to realize it had to belong to a Shetland."

"You mean, Sergeant Molinson doesn't know the shoe belongs to a Shetland?"

"No. Like I said, after he left, I was thinking about it. So I came in and checked our work records to see if we'd replaced a shoe for Mr. Pony while he was here. We hadn't. Nobody else I know of owns a Shetland. That pony has to be a transient."

"Oh, Honey, Davy Dodge owns a pony," Trixie bubbled.

"Which may have been auctioned," Honey argued. "Besides, how do we know someone didn't kidnap the pony along with the children? On the other hand, some other pony could have come down the path—not Wicky, and not Mr. Pony."

Regan looked thoughtful. "I'll tell you this— that Shetland belonged to somebody with money enough to take care of him and love enough to notice his particular need."

"There wasn't much money left at the Dodge farm, but there was certainly lots of love," Trixie declared. "If Davy owned a pony, his dad would take care of it."

"What does love have to do with it?" Honey asked.

"Like I said, this shoe wasn't factory made," explained Regan. "This fellow wore a corrective shoe. He toes in."

"You mean he looks kind of pigeon-toed?" Trixie asked.

Regan nodded. "Especially when he's barefoot."

"What if nobody had him reshod after he lost that shoe?" asked kindhearted Honey.

"They can take off the rest of the shoes. We let our horses go barefoot several weeks out of the year, you know. It keeps their frogs and horns in good condition." Regan glanced at his watch. "Got to go. Doc's coming to check teeth this morning. Jupe may have to have his teeth floated."

"Floated?" Trixie repeated. That horns and frogs were parts of the hoof, she knew. But what on earth was there in a horse's mouth that floated?

"His teeth might have to be filed down to an even level to help him grind his food," Regan explained.

"Not drilling!" Trixie cupped her own jaw in vivid recollection of her most recent trip to the dentist.

"More like cleaning," Regan said cheerfully as he disappeared into the barn.

Trixie helped Honey put the scrap back into the bin, then straightened and swiped a rusty hand across her damp forehead. It was such a hot day that the air danced.

"I've got a superdooper idea," she announced. "Let's go for a swim instead of taking a bath!"

"Luscious!" agreed Honey. "I'll have to dig out an extra suit for you."

"Let's just swim in our clothes," suggested Trixie. "We'd be dry by the time we got to my house. You can have lunch with me. We'll take care of Dodgy this afternoon and let his mother rest."

"Terrific," Honey chirped. "You can borrow one of our bicycles."

The girls coasted most of the way down the

well-beaten path to the lake. Within sight of the boathouse, Trixie noticed the blurred remains of hoofprints. "Have you ridden here since the rain?" she asked.

"No, I've been exercising Lady in the meadow," answered Honey.

"That reminds me," Trixie groaned. "I haven't exercised Susie in ages."

"Nothing's more important than taking care of Dodgy and finding Davy," her friend reassured her.

"Thanks for not saying 'trying to find,' " Trixie said soberly.

"You'll find him. You always do," Honey told her.

"*We* always do," Trixie corrected. Just then, she saw a fairly deep print on the side of the path. "I wish we had that horseshoe," she fretted. "That print looks like the right size."

All thoughts of horseshoes and kidnappers were temporarily shelved when the girls caught sight of the sparkling blue lake. They hopped about on the hot boards of the dock just long enough to remove their sneakers, then they dived in at the same time. By the third stroke, Honey had pulled ahead of Trixie.

119

After a few minutes of porpoiselike splashing and playing, Trixie decided, "I still feel sticky. I'm going to shore for the soap."

Honey flipped over and floated lazily. "Toss it to me when you're through."

Chunks of soap were kept in a covered plastic carton nailed to the edge of the dock. When Trixie reached for the top bar, she found that the bottom of it was wet. *That's odd*, she thought. There were drainage holes punched in the plastic carton. All the soap should be bone-dry.

Trixie waded back in, ducked under, lathered her arms, and ducked again. She was more thorough in her second lathering and took time to study the shores of the small lake, watching for movements. She saw none.

Trixie swam out far enough to lob the bar to Honey. "Has anybody been swimming this morning?" she asked.

"Not that I know of," Honey said as she lathered her own hands and arms. After she rinsed, she said, "Reflections from the water are going to give us a dandy sunburn pretty soon. We'd better go to shore."

Trixie pointed to the opposite side of the lake. "I see a nice shady spot where we could rest."

Honey agreed, and the girls paddled to shore, where they jumped from stone to stone until they found a rock large enough to stretch out on.

"I could stay here all day if I wasn't so hungry," sighed Trixie as she got herself comfortable.

"Me, too. The only thing is, we're not making things come out right," Honey complained. "Our sneakers and bicycles are at the boathouse, and the soap is over here."

"If Mart were here, he'd spout quotations," Trixie said.

"A rolling stone gathers no soap?" Honey suggested helpfully.

Trixie snorted, then recited triumphantly, "When we have not what we like, we must like what we have."

"I'll buy that," Honey declared.

For the moment, Trixie liked what she had. She lay on her stomach, chin propped on folded arms. Blue sky, tall pines, and flowing water combined to give her a feeling of total isolation. Lining the Hudson not far away were brickyards and cement factories, automotive assembly plants, railroads and highways. Here in the woods, the earth was undisturbed. Trixie liked it that way, especially when she had a puzzle

121

that needed to be worked out.

She squinted through sandy lashes, and the whole scene went slightly out of focus. A glare of light was bothersome. After a minute, she got up impatiently.

"Do we have to go now?" Honey asked. "I wasn't planning on moving a muscle for at least six months."

"I just want to pick up something over there," Trixie said. She sprinted into the woods to see what was littering one of her favorite spots. It turned out to be a glass bottle . . . with ounce-levels marked!

"Honey!" she shrieked. "I've found one of Dodgy's bottles!"

Honey waved a lazy hand. "Bobby must have carried off one of the baby's bottles to catch minnows or something," she mumbled.

Trixie ran back and squatted beside Honey. "This isn't one of the disposable bottles you bought. Honey, it's glass—and there's dried milk in the bottom!"

Honey was forced to pay attention. Suddenly she said, "If this *is* Dodgy's bottle, it means that whoever left him in the doghouse could still be hanging around."

"Jeepers!" whispered Trixie. "And the soap in the plastic carton was wet, like somebody'd used it."

Quietly the girls turned from side to side, searching for signs of another human being. They saw nothing, but Trixie urged, "Let's have a closer look."

Back she hopped to the edge of the lake. Carefully she examined the whole area. "There's crushed grass," she called to Honey, who was working her way toward the woods. "And some kind of pushed-in places. Come and look."

Honey obliged. It was she who found a dime and two pennies in the mashed grass. "Sit down here and put your heels in those little holes," she commanded.

"I see what you mean!" Trixie exclaimed. "Someone sat here by the brook and dug in his heels. He lost the coins out of his pockets. You know, I'll bet it was Davy who sat here and lost this money."

"Couldn't it have been the kidnapper?" Honey asked.

"The heel marks are too small for a grown man," Trixie countered. "Besides, don't you remember? Eileen said Davy broke some piggy

123

banks. Dimes and pennies are piggy-bank food!"

"But the kidnap note," Honey said earnestly. "We might be trailing a grown man, and a dangerous one at that."

Trixie gulped. "Well, let's take these things to Sergeant Molinson," she said, dropping the coins into the bottle. "He beat us to the horseshoe, but these discoveries should even the score."

"Oh, Trixie, you talk like this is a basketball game. This could be a life-and-death matter!"

"I know, I know," replied her friend. "That's why it's so important that we don't blow it by missing clues or something." Then she scowled with exasperation. "Now, how am I going to swim with this bottle?"

"Carry it in one hand and swim with the other," Honey said.

"And make the sergeant go purple with rage? No, I'm sure I've ruined some fingerprints already. I'll have to make a raft."

Trixie searched through the ground duff—the leaves, twigs, needles, dried grass, and fallen branches—until she came across a scrap of the blade of an oar, dry and white with age. "Instant raft," she announced.

Honey had waded back into the lake, and

Trixie soon followed, carefully pushing the oar with its cargo.

Once back at the boathouse, they decided to examine it. Honey unlocked the door, and together they stood just inside it. The shelves were stocked with summer sports equipment and various hardware items. Nothing seemed out of place. There were no tracks on the floor, and the locked windows didn't seem to have been tampered with.

Trixie let out a sigh. Half of her was relieved that the Wheeler property hadn't been invaded and that no one was likely to jump out of hiding. However, the sight of Davy Dodge in the boathouse would have been welcome.

Honey locked up the boathouse, and both girls put on their sneakers and started pedaling toward Crabapple Farm. Trixie carried the bottle and coins in her basket. She glanced back and noticed that Jim's huge beach towel was draped on the towel line. "We should have put that inside," she commented.

"Next time," Honey said. "It's okay where it is."

As they rode, the girls kept their eyes open and were soon rewarded by the sight of a pile of branches, leaves wilted, in the shape of a lopsided tepee. With a surge of excitement, Trixie flipped down the kickstand of her borrowed bicycle and ran across a glade sheltered by a great oak. Something white was visible underneath those branches. She bent down and yanked it out.

"Aw, just an old rag—" she began, then looked more closely. "Why, it's part of a T-shirt. It's the half that matches Dodgy's diaper!"

Honey caught up to her and agreed. "If we are following a kidnapper, he's the *oddest* one I ever heard of," Honey sighed as the two of them scouted the area around the oak tree. "You'd think he'd have stayed in a place where he could take care of a baby, instead of wandering around in the forest with a pony and no diapers."

" 'Wandering' is right," affirmed Trixie. "From the clues we're finding, it seems like whoever we're following is traveling around in circles— no direction whatsoever. This tepee is the weirdest clue yet. It's too small for Davy—or even for Dodgy."

"I don't know about that," said Honey, shuddering. "All I can think about is germs. How on earth could Dodgy have *survived?*"

"He must be a stronger baby than he seems," Trixie said.

"How could someone expect Dodgy to survive without supplies and without care?" Honey fretted.

"He didn't think," Trixie said, then flushed. The words were all too familiar. She heard variations of them practically every day of her life from her parents and her brothers. She even heard them from her friends if she plunged in over her head while working on a mystery. Was she looking for someone like herself, someone who acted first, then did the best he could to patch things up?

Or was she looking for a hardened criminal, someone vicious enough to abuse a tiny baby, kidnap a boy and his pony, and terrorize two young parents?

Twenty Thousand Dollars • 9

AFTER THEIR SEARCH had revealed no recogniz-able prints around the oak, the two girls stood close together, listening to the lazy midday sounds of insects, birds, and creaks of the forest as it shifted its weight in millions of impercep-tible movements.

"We'd better go home before we starve to death," Trixie declared finally. She tried to con-centrate on the task at hand—wobbling back over the ruts to Crabapple Farm.

"There's one point we've been overlooking," Honey said from behind her.

Instantly Trixie turned her whole attention to what Honey was saying.

"The rider couldn't have been far from a milk supply," Honey said. "Milk spoils fast in this weather."

"What a brilliant deduction," began Trixie. Then she almost fell off her bike. "Jeepers, there's a convention at our house!" Three extra cars were parked in the turnaround. Dan's Spartan munched grass along the orchard fence, and Jim's bicycle was propped against a porch post.

When the girls pedaled closer, they saw a picnic being organized in the backyard. Eileen and Di were setting the table. The three Belden boys, plus Jim and Dan, carried food that Mrs. Belden handed through an open kitchen window. Miss Goodley sat in a garden chair, writing her report with Dodgy on her lap. Observing Dodgy were Dr. Ferris and Sergeant Molinson, who in turn were closely watched by Reddy.

"My goodness!" Honey gasped. "What if— Do you suppose the police have found Davy, and we're the only ones who don't know?"

"I—I hope so," Trixie managed to gulp. She was too ashamed to admit the truth to Honey. How could she explain that she wanted to be the one who solved this mystery, who led a healthy boy to a pair of frantic parents?

"Slowpokes!" Di sang out.

"Coming," Honey called.

"What's going on?" Trixie asked when she came face-to-face with Mart and a huge tray of sandwiches.

"Other than an acute attack of inanition," replied her brother pompously, "not much. Everybody except you was still working here at noon, so Moms asked them all to stay for lunch."

Trixie was unaccustomed to munching salad while sitting between a doctor and a police sergeant. Nor was she used to facing a social worker while she ate a juicy sandwich. However, her hunger overcame her shyness.

"More salad?" she asked Miss Goodley, who nodded.

Mart went to the kitchen to refill the salad bowl. When he appeared again, he was trying to balance the bowl in one hand and a large pitcher of lemonade in the other.

Trixie ran to his aid. "What did you say you were having?" she asked sweetly. "An attack of the clumsies?"

"Help me, you fiend," growled Mart.

Trixie grabbed the heavy pitcher. By the time she and Mart made sure that everyone had more salad and lemonade, Dr. Ferris was speaking.

"You young people have done a great job with this baby," he said. "His weight is nearly back to normal, and those bruises and pin stabs are clearing up just fine."

Brian glanced over to where Dodgy's basket sat in the shade. "How do you think he got the bruises, sir? It's puzzling that they're just on his stomach and under his arms, and that they don't reach his back, don't you think?"

Dr. Ferris shook his white head. "I've seen a lot of battered children in my day. This one doesn't fit the pattern. His injuries are neither serious nor permanent, and there's nothing to suggest that abuse took place prior to his present bruises. It's my opinion that those bruises were accidental and inflicted quite recently."

"But he's so thin!" Trixie burst out. She blushed. Who was she to argue with a doctor who'd dealt with injuries most of his life?

Dr. Ferris didn't seem to mind a difference of opinion. "At this age, weight seems to fall away overnight when something goes wrong," he explained. "Weight can be regained just as quickly.

He's an alert, strong infant. He'll be plump and rosy in no time."

Eileen Dodge smiled widely while winking back tears.

Trixie turned to the sergeant. "Any news about Davy?"

"I followed up on that tip you gave me about the horseshoe. I had a farrier check it. It belongs to a Shetland."

"I know," Trixie said impatiently.

The sergeant raised an eyebrow. "We're checking out the Shetlands in the area to make certain the shoe belongs to Wicky." He helped himself to sliced tomatoes and glanced at his watch. "I'm standing by for a call from Saw Mill River. It may be from David Dodge."

"Oh, I hope so," Eileen began, then added hesitantly, "I—I think."

She looked so frightened by the possibility of bad news that Trixie offered the first consolation she could think of—the morning's discoveries. She fetched them and, with Honey's help, told the story of the search they had made.

"Is this Dodgy's bottle?" the sergeant asked Eileen.

"Oh, yes. At least, I have bottles like that left

132

from Davy's baby days. But I don't recognize the label in the neck of that torn T-shirt. My husband doesn't wear that brand. And, of course, I have no way of identifying the coins."

Even the sergeant had to admit that the girls had spent their morning profitably. "I'll get these things to the lab right away. It just may be that Davy is still hanging around the woods." He paused to look sternly at Trixie and Honey. "Just keep in mind that he may or may not be alone."

The kitchen phone rang persistently. Mart loped across the yard and porch to answer. He didn't take time to return to the table with a message but instead shouted from the kitchen window, "Sergeant, it's your Saw Mill River call!"

Trixie debated about whether or not to follow the sergeant. Finally she told herself, "This is our case, too," and beckoned to Honey. The two girls stood just inside the kitchen door.

"Read it to me, Mr. Dodge," the sergeant was saying. "Slowly."

Trixie watched him write while he repeated aloud, " 'Are your kids worth twenty thousand dollars? Then prove it.' " The sergeant prepared to continue writing, then looked startled. "That's

133

all?" he barked. "Well, sit tight and keep in touch with me. We have a few new clues here, but nothing definite yet. No, I think it's safer if I don't try to contact you till we know for sure what's going on. Keep your chin up. By the way, your wife and baby are just fine. They send their love."

Again Trixie felt a little thrill of surprise at the sergeant's real concern for the emotional welfare of the people he served. Always before, she'd regarded him as a hardheaded, grouchy cop.

As the three made their way back to the picnic table, it seemed to Trixie that she saw Eileen's shadow stretch a bit too far. For one instant, Trixie had the impression that a second shadow blended with Eileen's. How else could Dodgy's beautiful mother, slim to the point of leanness, cast a lumpy-looking shadow? Trixie shook her head till her curls bounced, shut her eyes, and looked again. Eileen's shadow was long and lean again. *I'm seeing things*, she decided.

Almost at once, she heard a kind of thump and slither. No one else seemed to notice, although the robins darted into the maple tree by the doghouse. She assumed that the burden of the

Dodge case was affecting her senses. *Stay alert,* she warned herself.

Sergeant Molinson spoke to Dr. Ferris in a low mutter. The doctor kept his eyes on Eileen while the sergeant told her about the second note, then he reached across the table to test her pulse.

Eileen jerked her wrist away and made knots of her two hands. "I'm fine! It's Davy we have to worry about!" She widened her large blue eyes at the sergeant. "Did you say twenty thou— Why, we'll only have a few dollars left from our auction when we pay that! And we have so many bills!"

Trixie noticed that Eileen did not say "if." She said "when." Of course her boys were worth twenty thousand dollars.

Boys. Not boy.

"Sergeant!" Trixie shouted. "That kidnapper's a fake! He doesn't know we have Dodgy, and he probably doesn't even know where Davy is!"

"You caught on to that, too, huh?" the sergeant snapped. "The note said 'kids.' I was on the verge of calling in the FBI, but now I see it won't be necessary. What we have here is some two-bit, small-time swindler who's trying to cash

135

in on one family's troubles!" His voice was full of contempt. Turning to Eileen, he asked, "You *sure* you don't know anyone who would fit that description?"

"Oh, no!" Eileen said fiercely.

The sergeant thanked Mrs. Belden for lunch and got ready to leave. Miss Goodley and Dr. Ferris rose to follow him.

"Honey and I will keep looking for Davy," Trixie promised. "Just Davy."

"Just don't go looking for the would-be kidnapper," the sergeant stressed. "This wretch might find out that Dodgy's back. No kids, no easy money. In that case, he might try to pull some kind of stunt."

"Oh, please be careful," Eileen begged, turning from Trixie to Honey.

"We'll find him," Trixie said stubbornly.

As the three cars disappeared down the lane and Eileen and Mrs. Belden started clearing the table, Jim turned to Trixie and his sister. "You have the Bob-Whites to help you, you know."

Brian nodded vigorously. "Davy has to find food," he said earnestly. "Maybe he'll return to the places where he was able to find food during the past few days." He winked soberly at his small brother. "Just like Bobby returns to the cookie jar until he finds it empty."

"What about checking out the nearby milk supplies to see where Dodgy was fed?" Honey urged. "Davy must have eaten, too."

"Let's do that later," suggested Trixie. "While it's still light, I think we should all concentrate on finding the Shetland. We can cover a lot of territory in two or three hours and exercise the horses at the same time. When we find the pony, we may find the boy."

"I agree with Trixie," said Jim. "I'll go on ahead to the stables and start saddling the horses." And he hurried away, walking to save time on the uphill bicycle path.

"Where will we start?" objected Di. "I mean, I want to help, but it seems so hopeless."

Dan spoke up quietly. "We start in the clearing where Spartan grazes." In response to everyone's look of astonishment, he went on, "The other day, I noticed that the tools on Mr. Maypenny's workbench were out of order, so I've been keeping my eyes open for trespassers. Just before I came to lunch today, I found three horseshoes and a pile of nails by a stump in the clearing, plus Mr. Maypenny's missing rasp."

137

"Well, what are we waiting for?" bellowed Mart as he jumped to his feet.

"Shouldn't we help your mother first?" Honey asked reluctantly.

"Not at all," called Eileen. "I'll take care of that. After all, it's my son you're hunting for."

As Trixie turned to leave, she noticed that Bobby was busily wrapping a sandwich in a paper napkin. "I'm helping, too," he explained. "In case Davy's hungry, I'm putting this sandwich on top of the doghouse."

"You know, he may have something there," Brian said.

Trixie thought so, too. Oh, if only she could be in two places at the same time! She knew she had to join the search party for the pony, though; there were few enough searchers as it was. Oh, well. Bobby would be so proud if his sandwich happened to lure Davy into the yard.

Within an hour, the Bob-Whites and their horses were gathering at the clearing. As Di cantered in on Sunny, she said apprehensively, "Oh, I feel so sorry for Eileen. If anything like this ever happened to the twins, I'd just go insane with worry!"

"Nothing like this could ever happen to your

brothers and sisters," Honey reassured her.

When Dan showed them where he had found the shoes, Trixie commented, "This is quite a way from where I found the other shoe."

Dan shrugged. "A horse can wander pretty far while grazing. In the forest, it's sometimes a long way between mouthfuls of tender grass. He's probably a grain-fed animal, not much used to foraging for himself."

"Probably hungry, too," Brian added. "Come on. Let's start looking for Shetland tracks. If you find something, yell."

Soon after the riders scattered, everybody was yelling. Each yell was almost immediately followed by a groan. The pony had done a lot of wandering, but the tracks were next to impossible to follow in the forest duff.

Trixie took time out to study the land that surrounded the clearing. The area sloped uphill in one direction and downhill in the other. Wouldn't the pony have taken the easiest route and moved downward? After a fruitless few minutes, she decided there was something wrong with her thinking. Maybe a horse would stay on level ground as long as the grass held out. That theory should be easy to test.

Trixie let Susie pick her own way, and sure enough, Susie took the course of least resistance. Gradually the mare's neat hooves scribed a wide arc that led to the grounds of Ten Acres. The ruins of the Frayne mansion had stood here in hollow neglect since the fire that had resulted in Jim's inheritance of his great-uncle's wealth and his adoption by the Wheelers. The barn had not burned, but it, too, had fallen into disrepair. With a growing excitement, Trixie rode through the weed-choked barnyard and on to the barn itself.

Yes! There were visible prints near a sagging door, and those small hoof marks toed in!

Positive that she had found the Shetland, Trixie guided Susie into the silent barn. She was just about to dismount, when to her horror, something swished past her head.

A Goat Named Nancy • 10

AFTER A STARTLED INSTANT, Trixie realized that she'd disturbed a bat, which had moved past her into the dim heights of the loft. Once her heart had stopped pounding and her eyes had grown used to the darkness, she also realized that the bat was the only living thing housed in the barn. There was no pony and no small boy, although there was evidence that the Shetland had been there.

Trixie spent a long time riding in and out among the trees and bushes surrounding the ruins. Finding nothing, but sure she was on the right track, she eventually headed back to the Manor House stables. Honey, Jim, Mart, and Brian were already there.

"Di rode Sunny home, and Dan had to go back to work," Brian told Trixie gloomily. "None of us found a thing."

"Trixie, you look like the cat that swallowed the canary," Mart accused. "Or should I say the shamus that swallowed the Shetland?"

Honey eyed her partner. "Trixie, you *did* find something."

Eyes shining, Trixie told about the tracks she had found at the barn. "I think Davy and Wicky use it as a hideaway. Maybe they go back there at night," she finished.

"Could be," agreed Jim.

"Well, there's only one way to prove it," Brian declared. "The thing to do is to explore the Frayne place after dark. If we do it tonight, we might not have to backtrack on checking out the milk supply."

"Have dinner with us so we can get an early start," Honey urged.

Trixie began an objection. "Oh, but I'm so hot and dusty."

"Okay, let me change that invitation," Jim

142

said. "How about a shower, *then* dinner?"

"You're out of luck, Jim," Mart put in. "My sister has a proclivity toward thunderstorms, not showers, as a means of expunging dirt."

"Ah, now I remember," teased Jim. "Rather primitive, I think, yet effective. I mean, she seldom looks as bad as she does now."

"Speak for yourself!" Trixie sputtered.

"I think we all need showers," Honey spoke up tactfully.

The others laughingly agreed, and by the time they joined Mr. and Mrs. Wheeler and Miss Trask for dinner, the five were scrubbed till they shone. They were hungry, too.

"Sheer luxury!" Trixie gloated. "No dishes to wash."

No discussion with Dad about auctions, either, she thought ruefully a second later. Maybe, just maybe, there would turn out to be no need for that talk.

A beautiful sunset was beginning to spill across the sky by the time the young people finished their strawberry tortes and dashed outside to the Bob-White station wagon. Jim guided the big car through the tall dry weeds around Ten Acres without mishap. A thorough search of the grounds on foot made it clear that the abandoned property hid neither Davy nor a pigeon-toed pony.

"Nothing like getting tangled up in cobwebs right after a shower," Jim grumbled good-naturedly as they returned to the station wagon.

"Well, that's an hour wasted," sighed Brian.

"The clock upbraids me with the evanescence of hours," Mart intoned.

"Oh, Mart, cut the gibberish," Trixie pleaded. "We've got to figure out where Dodgy would have got his milk."

"I know," Mart said soberly. "I'm just trying not to have a nervous breakdown in the meantime. What about Lytell's store? Seems like a logical place to start."

"Davy could have bought some with the money from the piggy banks," Honey agreed.

Jim suggested stopping in at the houses between Ten Acres and the store, but at none of them had anybody been asked to fill a baby's milk bottle.

Mr. Lytell was the neighborhood gossip. Behind his wire-rimmed glasses, his pale eyes brightened with curiosity at Trixie's query about a small boy buying milk. "Would that have some-

144

thing to do with that baby up at your house?" he asked.

"Sort of," Trixie answered noncommittally.

The storekeeper shrugged. "Can't say. A lot of people buy milk here."

Trying not to become discouraged, Trixie returned to the car and recommended checking at Glen Road Inn next. There they found Ella Kline enjoying the evening coolness on the lawn, her wheelchair parked near a hedge of lilac bushes. She waved and called to them. After greetings were exchanged, the pretty seamstress reached for Trixie's hand. "I've been meaning to call you—I found out about that fly sheet."

Mart smote his brow. "Don't tell me they're letting rooms to horses!"

Ella twinkled at Mart. "Only on the first floor. Horses aren't allowed on the stairs."

"Flies are allowed anywhere?" Jim teased.

Trixie leaned toward Ella. "What about the fly sheet?"

Ella pointed. "See a kind of hidden place in those shrubs by the gate? Pete told me he found the fly sheet there, folded up neatly."

Trixie ambled over to the gate and noticed that the lawn hadn't been mowed right up to the shrubs and trees. An object could remain hidden there for quite a while. Even though the inn was a former manor house, it had seen better days and had known better care. Trixie dropped to her knees to paw through the branches and tall grass.

Jim hurried to join her. "Here, let me do that. You'll get bitten by spiders."

"Since when are you immune to spiders?" Trixie retorted.

"I'm not, but the stick I poke with is," Jim said.

While the others chatted with Ella, Jim and Trixie went over the ground near the gate thoroughly. At last Trixie sat back on her heels, ready to admit defeat. That was when she saw something dangling in a forsythia bush a few yards away. It turned out to be a scrap of blue yarn.

"I'll be darned," Jim said. "It's a . . . what-you-call-it . . ."

"A bootee!" Trixie said with a quiver of excitement. As if she'd needed it, this was more solid proof that Dodgy and the horse were connected. But where was the third member of this triangle? She and Jim searched further, but there were no more clues to be found.

When they returned to the group on the lawn,

they learned that Brian had talked to the cook. No one had asked to have a bottle filled, but several days ago, a boy had paid for one glass of milk and carried it to the courtyard to drink.

"Davy," Trixie breathed.

"He must have poured the milk into Dodgy's bottle," Honey agreed.

Trixie and Honey took one last look around the forsythia bush before the Bob-Whites said good night to Ella.

"Where to now?" Jim asked when they were back in the station wagon.

Trixie was too deep in frustrated thought to reply, so Jim swung the car onto Old Telegraph Road. "We could try some of the houses this way," he decided.

With the lowering of the sun, a glow had spread over the land. Trixie tilted her face to the breeze coming in through the window. Suddenly she pointed and exclaimed, "There!"

"Huh?" Jim asked.

"Tar!" Trixie shrieked.

"An odorous, bituminous, viscous liquid, according to Webster," Mart began calmly. Then he, too, waved his arms and yelled, "Turn around!"

147

"Brian, does being nuts run in your family?" Jim demanded.

"We found some tar on Dodgy's foot," Brian reminded him.

"Well, give me some warning this time," Jim said as he pulled to the side of the road.

"You'll be able to smell it," Trixie said.

Jim had to retrace only a few hundred yards before Trixie shouted, "Stop!"

Facing the protected forest of the Wheeler game preserve stood an old Dutch barn, which was apparently being remodeled. Jim peered through the dusk to see that the contractor's sign included the name of a well-known Hudson River artist. "Wow, what a studio!" he exclaimed.

Trixie wasn't looking at the carefully placed windows. She was looking at a tethered goat. "Milk!" she squealed.

"Shall we explore?" prompted Brian.

They found the usual construction clutter: stacks of lumber, a temporary tool shed that was locked, empty nail kegs, sawhorses, and several empty tar buckets. Jim whistled while they completed a quick tour of the ancient farm lot. "Wow," he said again. "When I have my school, I hope I can find a solid old barn like this to fix

148

up for a craft building." Jim was planning to use his inheritance to build a camplike school for underprivileged children.

Mart, like Trixie, was more interested in the goat than in the barn. "They're using the goat to get rid of the brush that's grown up around the lot," he commented.

The group heard a noise behind them and turned to find a tall boy, wearing shorts and sneakers, biking onto the lot. He dropped one foot to the ground and looked them over, obviously curious. Because he wore no shirt, Trixie guessed he lived nearby. She introduced herself and added anxiously, "We're on the trail of a Shetland that might have been here several days ago."

"Black? Very small?" the boy asked.

Trixie gulped. "When did you see him?" she asked breathlessly.

"Last Monday or Tuesday—I'm not sure which —I found the pony playing tag with Nancy." He nodded toward the goat. Hearing her name, Nancy stopped munching alfalfa and stepped forward daintily. The boy scratched her velvety ears while he talked.

"The pony got his foot caught in a coil of

heavy chain. I was trying to free him when a kid came rushing across the road to help me. He was awfully nervous about something. A couple of times, he ran back into the woods over there." The teen-ager waved toward the trees of the game preserve. "He looked hungry, so I asked him if he'd like a cup of goat milk. He didn't drink all of it. He asked if he could bring the cup back later. I told him sure, and if he wanted more, just to help himself."

"He knew how to milk?" Brian asked.

"Sure, doesn't everybody?" the boy asked, grinning.

"Not I," Brian said, "and I live on a farm. I just don't happen to have a speaking acquaintance with a goat." At that moment, the goat bunted Brian's leg.

"Now you have," needled Mart. "Say how-de-doo!"

The boy whizzed away on his bicycle, and Trixie sighed. "It's too dark to search the woods now, but I'm certainly coming back tomorrow. Are you free, Honey?"

"Wild horses couldn't keep me at home," Honey answered.

"Mart and I have a lot of work on the farm

tomorrow," Brian said, "so that leaves us out."

"Regan's tied up with dental checkups at the stables," Jim said, "so I have to do the routine chores. It may be noon before I'm free to drive us here."

"We could ride Susie and Lady," Honey ventured hesitantly.

"That's a pretty wild trail cutting through the heart of the preserve," objected Jim.

"We can bicycle," Trixie declared sturdily. "But now let's get home so we can get some rest first." In the middle of a yawn, she remembered that Jim had left his bicycle at Crabapple Farm. "May I ride your ten-speed tomorrow, Jim?"

Jim grinned. "Sure, just don't get arrested for speeding."

Mart whooped, and Jim went on, "You think I'm kidding? Sergeant Molinson threatened to give me a speeding ticket if he ever caught me riding on a public highway the way we go down the bicycle trail."

When they got home, the young Beldens found their parents silently relaxing on the dark porch. Only the creaking of the porch swing betrayed their presence.

Mrs. Belden went inside to mix the dough for

the next day's bread baking, and Brian and Mart soon followed her.

Trixie slumped down on a porch step and began running clues through her mind.

"You had a phone call from Molinson," her father informed her. "Another note came, this time with instructions about leaving the money."

"How can they do that?" Trixie cried. "We have the baby, and Davy's taking care of himself. We haven't found one shred of evidence to indicate that a man's been traveling with him."

Who could possibly be trying to collect twenty thousand dollars from the Dodges, a sum that would leave them practically bankrupt? *Wait a minute*, thought Trixie, jerking herself upright. *There's something awfully peculiar about that sum. It's not a very large amount for a ransom, for one thing. For another thing, who would know that the Dodges managed to collect that amount at their auction? Jeepers, it has to be someone connected with the auction itself!* Suddenly, she remembered that she hadn't had a chance to ask her father about the auction process.

"Dad," Trixie pleaded, "will you tell me how an auction works, please?"

Her father answered after a thoughtful pause. "Well, an auction is a pretty cut-and-dried affair, regulated by law. An auctioneer is bonded to ensure his honesty, and he pays for a license. He can be fined or have his license revoked if he doesn't obey the law, so he has to be very careful about the clerks he hires."

"They're the ones who keep the records?" asked Trixie.

"Right. There's an inventory list that shows what's to be sold, and a sales record that lists what actually was sold. You see, a sale isn't complete until the auctioneer says 'Sold!' and taps his desk with his gavel. A bid is an offer, but the drop of the gavel changes that bid to a contract. That means the seller has to sell and the buyer has to buy."

"What about fraud?" Trixie guessed shrewdly. Her feeling was mounting that there was some kind of chicanery connected with the Dodge auction.

"Some people are greedy," Peter Belden conceded. "A dummy bidder might raise the honest bid. The seller might get someone to bid in on something that wasn't selling for enough. Stolen goods may be sold. A lot of things can happen.

153

Still, our laws do a pretty good job of keeping auction cheating under control."

"Suppose . . ." Trixie's voice trembled with the weight of a brand-new idea, the way a branch trembles when a bird drops down to rest.

"When you begin to suppose, Trixie, anything can happen," her father sighed.

"Just suppose," Trixie persisted, "there's somebody connected with the auction who does get greedy. He knows just about how much money the family's goods can be sold for, so he decides to kidnap their children and ask for that exact amount of money."

"Then what?" prompted Mr. Belden.

"I—I don't know what happens next," Trixie admitted. "Dad, did the sergeant say when the ransom money was to be delivered?"

"The note said Saturday night at nine o'clock."

"Tomorrow night?" Trixie wailed. "Yipes! That gives us just one day to—"

Her father interrupted. "In your hypothetical case, I suppose you realize that the logical persons to suspect are the clerks. Now, you know you can't go around making charges without proof. If the clerks are innocent, they can sue you. If they're guilty, you put yourself in danger along with those hypothetical children." Peter Belden became more serious by the second. "I strongly advise you to call Molinson if that brain of yours is cooking up a plan to see those clerks." Then he leaned forward and captured both her hands. "Trixie, where *did* you get this great lump of curiosity that keeps all of us in hot water?"

"Same place Brian and Mart got theirs about medicine and agriculture, I guess."

Her father sighed. "But their interests don't keep getting them in trouble."

Trixie said good night and went inside, her head whirling with all the new information. She paused in the kitchen doorway.

Her mother wrapped a large bowl of dough with a linen towel and said, "Penny for your thoughts, dear."

"Oh, Moms, I just this minute realized how awful it will be to give up Dodgy." Trixie's voice came out weak and lonely, like the wail of a lost child. She decided to stop in the guest room to kiss Dodgy good night. An instant later, she came darting back to the kitchen.

"Moms, where is he?" she gasped. "His basket is gone!"

155

Smitty's T-Shirt · 11

RELAX, TRIXIE," her mother admonished. "Eileen felt that she had to go home for the weekend in case her house is being watched. So we drove her there, and she left Dodgy in our care. Brian took the basket to his room for the night."

"Brian has to get up early to work in the fields tomorrow," Trixie recalled. "He needs his sleep. I'll take Dodgy to my room."

Mrs. Belden disagreed. "Brian can afford to miss sleep once in a while. If he wants to share this night with a sleeping baby, let him. That's part of his growing up. Someday a child who is

156

desperately ill may live because Brian Belden learned to put a baby's comfort ahead of his own."

Trixie heard tears as well as pride in her mother's voice. "Brian's growing up too fast already!" she stormed. "So's everybody!" She whirled around and went upstairs to her own room.

Change. She didn't mind it, except when it adversely affected people and places she loved. Because she had learned to love Dodgy, she had to get his family reunited. He must grow up with the same kind of family love that she knew. But how could she do all that in one day?

"I must!" she muttered fiercely.

She was already into her pajamas before she decided that her father was right about calling Sergeant Molinson. After she'd dialed the number on the hall phone, she anticipated the sergeant's reaction.

Sure enough, he was impatient. "This better be important. I'm at work, you know."

"So am I," retorted Trixie. "I have more clues about Davy."

"Okay," he barked. "By the way, the lab tests proved that Davy handled that baby bottle. Of course, we had to separate his prints from some I'm sure were yours. Next time, use gloves. All right, fire away."

Trixie, thankful that he wasn't there to see her flushed cheeks, gave him a detailed report of the clues they'd found. She hesitated, then finished boldly, "Now I'd like to know the names of the people who handled the Dodge auction."

"Durham and Durham, Elmer and Mike," the sergeant said tersely. "Their clerks are Jeff and Roger Higgins."

"Where do they live?"

"In Sleepyside. David Dodge does all his business in Sleepyside. Don't concern yourself with them. We've had a tail on Elmer Durham ever since this case broke. So far as we can tell, he's clean, and so's his organization."

"Including the clerks?" Trixie asked.

"Jeff Higgins has been in the business as long as I've been on the police force. He's training his son now. They're bonded."

"That doesn't keep them honest forever," Trixie said.

"True. In fact, we're finding out that Roger Higgins may not be the solid citizen we know his father to be. Steer clear of the whole bunch!

Oh, and by the way, congratulations on making the connection with the auction."

"Thank you," Trixie said. "I got to thinking how strange it was to ask for twenty thousand from a man going broke, when there are so many kids in mansions in this area. Seems to me it must be someone not used to thinking about money in large amounts, but not above grabbing for all he can get."

"Mmm" was the police officer's noncommittal answer.

When Trixie hung up, she said the same thing. She'd have to store all these tidbits until the next day. She was certainly too exhausted to think any more that night.

For the first time, Dodgy slept through his night feeding. He let the household know it, loud and clear, right on the dot of six o'clock the next morning.

Trixie woke up when Brian's feet hit the floor with a thump. She rushed to help. "You get Dodgy's milk, and I'll dress him," she offered, taking the baby from his basket.

By this time, Dodgy was strong enough to empty his bottle in ten minutes. Brian set the basket in a protected area by the kitchen hutch.

Every Belden stopped by the basket to smile and coo at Dodgy even before they greeted each other. The by now familiar morning routine made Trixie's heart hurt when she thought of the Dodges.

She felt herself balancing on a high teeter-totter. She knew Dodgy could not be left alone for a minute. On the other hand, she simply had to make that trip to the old Dutch barn as soon as possible. It would take forever to get to the barn on a bicycle. To make a decent search was going to take even more time. *How* was she to manage?

While Trixie fretted, the telephone rang. Mart took the call. It was Di. From his expression, it was apparent that she was asking if she could come for breakfast. "Dost thou need a chariot?" he asked finally.

Evidently not, for he hung up an instant later. Then he reported the conversation, ending with, "She said she doesn't eat much, so don't dither, Moms." Instead of pulling out his chair, he tilted it backward between his long legs and dropped onto it with a plop. With no lost motion, his right hand reached for the toast, his left for the honeypot.

"Good coordination," remarked Peter Belden dryly.

Mart frowned critically. "But lacking in finesse," he decided.

His mother lifted runaway blond curls from her warm brow, cast an amused glance at the little scene, and reached for her breadboard.

Suddenly a load was lifted from Trixie's shoulders. Di was coming! She would take care of Dodgy and love every minute of it.

Without waiting for Di to arrive, Trixie gulped down her breakfast and went to call Honey. Then she went outside to wait for her. Unexpectedly, Honey arrived with Jim in the Bob-White station wagon.

"I thought you had to work at the stable," Trixie said to Jim.

"I did," he answered, "but I got up a few hours early. When I thought of all the miles you were going to have to pedal, I decided I could miss some sleep and help you out."

"I'm so glad," Trixie said earnestly. "We have a deadline—nine o'clock tonight."

Briefly she filled in Honey and Jim on her latest theory about the would-be kidnapper having something to do with the auction.

"Sounds like a reasonable hypothesis," Honey agreed slowly.

Trixie sighed. "Dad said something like that, too."

"He meant, and we mean," Jim said, "that you've made several assumptions that remain to be proved. As I see it, the sooner we find Davy, the better off everyone will be."

"Jim's right," said Honey, starting to get back inside the station wagon. "The Dodge children's safety is the most important thing."

"Okay," said Trixie, "but now how am I going to explain to Moms why I can't do my chores this morning? She's so busy that she won't even have time to listen to my very good excuse."

Instantly Honey turned around. "You won't have to bother her," she said. "We'll help you with your work, won't we, Jim?"

With three people doing the work of one, it wasn't long before Jim was pulling into the weed-grown driveway of the Dutch barn on Old Telegraph Road. Even on a Saturday morning, the lot was full of activity. Hammers banged, machinery whined, and men shouted. Jim spotted the foreman and walked over to him, hand outstretched. "Jim Frayne, Glen Road."

"Oh, sure. Smitty, here. I remember you, young fellow. My men put the new roof on the Manor House stables a few months back. What can I do for you?"

This was easier than Trixie had expected. She stepped forward to say, "We're hunting for a small boy and a black Shetland. Have you seen them?"

Smitty pushed his visored cap to the back of his head. "Not for several days. The kid seemed to have his hands full keeping track of that rascal. He had his mind on something back there in the woods."

Smitty shook his head. "I haven't been able to get that kid out of my mind. He seemed hungry, but he wouldn't ask for a bite of food if it killed him. It got so that the men would leave parts of sandwiches, apples, stuff like that, and tell him he'd do them a favor by eating the stuff. They told him they didn't want bees buzzing around the scraps in their lunch pails. I thought about calling the cops and asking them if somebody was looking for a missing kid, but, well—I guess I just never got around to it."

"Did you give him milk?" Trixie asked.

"Come to think of it, he did ask to buy goat

milk. Naturally I told him to help himself. The goat works here, same as we do. She's our scrub remover."

Smitty grinned. "You've heard about a goat's strange appetite? Well, I never did put much stock in that. You know, tin cans and all. Now? Well, I don't know. I left a T-shirt on a saw-horse, and it disappeared slicker'n a whistle. The only culprit I could see was Nancy!"

Trixie and Honey exchanged a knowing glance, and Trixie decided against telling Smitty that his T-shirt had wrapped a baby's bottom.

Friends of Moses White · 12

D<small>ID YOU EVER SEE</small> a man with the boy?" Honey asked.

"No, miss, he was a loner." A carpenter called for help, and Smitty walked away, shouting, "Hope you find that kid. His pony was a friendly little devil. Wouldn't mind having him for my kids!"

Trixie, Honey, and Jim called their thanks to Smitty and headed into the woods across from the barn.

"Let's fan out," Trixie said. "Davy's camp must have been close to the road, or else he couldn't have run back and forth when the pony's foot was caught in the chain."

The pitiful little camp was not that hard to find. A heap of boughs, all of them small enough to break by hand, had been arranged like a big bird's nest.

"Poor little kids," Honey mourned.

"Smart little kids," Jim corrected. "See? Food for the pony."

A clean spring bubbled in a tiny rock grotto and trickled away into a swale of lush green grass. A bottle had been left in the spring, propped up so that it was washed by running water. A diaper was caught in a bush nearby, and the second blue bootee was discovered in the nest.

"Something scared them out of here," Jim surmised thoughtfully.

"Or some*one*," Trixie said. "Come on, let's go to Sleepyside."

Jim observed the familiar gleam in her eyes. "Uh-oh," he said. "I have this feeling you're going to hunt up those auctioneers."

"But the sergeant said to stay away from them," said Honey, looking alarmed. "Besides, I thought we decided to concentrate on finding

Davy, not on searching for crooks."

"Finding Wicky will make it easy to find Davy," Trixie reminded her. "If we can see that auction book, that will tell us if Wicky was auctioned and who might have him. Anyway, even the sergeant said that Elmer Durham was honest. What harm could there be in just talking to the man, when we might learn something very important?"

Jim and Honey looked doubtful. Finally Jim said, "Well, I can see you're determined to go, and we're not about to let you walk into something alone, are we, Honey?"

"I guess not," Honey agreed.

"Thanks, you guys," said Trixie, already on her way back to the car.

Jim stopped the car at Wimpy's so Trixie could check the auctioneer's address in the phone book. Something made her also jot down the Balsam Street address of the two clerks.

Elmer Durham lived in a more than comfortable house in a beautiful residential area. Well-clipped lawns and hedges, riots of color in flower beds, and a fountain tossing rainbows gave no hint of mystery or crime.

A maid in a blue and white uniform asked the

three young people to wait on an antique bench in a square hall. Each piece of furniture, from the oriental rugs to the gilt-framed mirror, was gorgeous. Trixie wondered silently if all auctioneers were this rich.

Except for the gaudy rings on his fingers, the man who came to greet them looked like any businessman from Main Street. His hair was thinning at the temples, he wore glasses, and he had teeth so perfect they had to be dentures. He bit off the tip of a cigar as he walked forward.

The auctioneer shook their hands as the Bob-Whites introduced themselves. Unsmiling, he asked, "May I get you something to drink?"

"No, thank you," Trixie said quickly. She saw at once that the man was not going to make this easy. "We're, uh, looking for a Shetland pony."

"Looking for" seemed to be a magic phrase for the auctioneer. The words meant business, and business meant money. "I have no Shetland listed for immediate auction, but I can scout around for one for you," he said.

"No," Trixie said, "I mean that we're hunting for a pony you may have sold."

The man looked wary. "I don't deal in stolen goods. You're barking up the wrong tree."

"No, no!" Trixie said, shaking her curls. "We want to know if the Dodges sold their Shetland at their auction." She gulped and plunged on, watching his face. "A friend of ours, er, Moses White, would very much like to get in touch with the person who might have bought the black pony."

Trixie heard both Jim and Honey exhale slowly and carefully.

"Oh, *that* pony." Elmer Durham lit his cigar and puffed smoke that rose like a mushroom-shaped cloud around his head. "I have no immediate recollection of what it brought or who bought it, but it must have gone on the block. I recall listing it."

"Do—do you have a copy of the inventory and sales record?" Trixie asked, trying not to sound anxious.

"Jeff Higgins keeps the files," he replied.

Trixie was silent, wondering if she dared let this man know she recognized the name.

Durham assumed that she didn't and explained politely, "My clerk."

"Would he let us see the Dodge file?" Trixie asked.

The auctioneer blew another cloud of smoke

169

and shrugged. "Why not?" he asked, more of himself than of his callers.

Having reached this point in her investigation, Trixie decided she couldn't take the risk of having the door slammed in her face. "Would you please give us a note to show Mr. Higgins?" she asked.

Elmer Durham unclipped a pen from his shirt pocket, rummaged through his pants pockets for a piece of paper, and scrawled a note. Then he handed it to Trixie, who, pretending to be casual, folded it and put it into her pocket without glancing at it.

As they returned to the car, being careful not to walk too fast, Honey said, "I don't think I care for him."

"He certainly didn't know what to make of us," declared Jim.

"He must have decided we were harmless," Trixie said, patting her pocket. She waited until Jim had pulled away from the curb before snatching the paper from her pocket. "It's on his official stationery!" she exulted. Then she read aloud, " 'Jeff, let these kids see the Dodge file. They're friends of Moses White. Know him?' " The note was signed, "El."

Honey looked proud. "Moses White—that was pretty clever, Trixie."

"Let's just hope we didn't open a can of worms," Jim said. "Wouldn't it be cute if there were a real person with that name?"

By that time, they had reached Balsam, which was the first street east of Hawthorne, in Sleepyside's least desirable neighborhood. Trixie looked about uneasily and edged closer to Jim as they went up the Higginses' walk. Honey was already holding Jim's arm.

At the end of the walk was an ordinary square duplex split down the middle, with a door on each side of the railing that cut the narrow front porch in half. A dingy card coated with plastic showed that Jeff Higgins lived in apartment A.

The man who answered the door wore trifocal glasses and had ink on his hands. *He doesn't look like a criminal,* thought Trixie. Jeff Higgins simply looked worn out.

And so did his living room, Trixie discovered when he invited them in while he read Elmer Durham's note.

"Excuse me," he said. "I'll get the Dodge file."

While he was gone, a younger man stepped

over the porch divider rail and came in through the screen door with an opened can of beer. He shouted, "Hey, Pop, I want to borrow your—" Then he stopped in his tracks at the sight of the three visitors.

Trixie never did find out what he wanted to borrow. He plopped down on the arm of a threadbare davenport and stared at them. Roger Higgins was larger than his father, with a great brush of brown hair, a moustache, and a bushy beard. There were puffs under his eyes and a bulge over his belt. This definitely wasn't his first can of beer.

Jeff Higgins came back into the room, ruffling through papers.

"Whatcha got there?" the younger man asked.

"Keep your shirt on, Rog," Jeff said. "These people want to see the Dodge papers."

"They can't do that," Roger said, scowling.

"Oh, yes, they can," his father said mildly, handing Jim the folder.

Roger Higgins snatched for it as it passed in front of him but missed. "Hey, Pop, aren't you even asking for identification?"

"Here's El's note," Jeff said, handing it to Roger. Then he left the room.

Quickly Jim put in, "I'm Jim Frayne. This is my sister, Madeleine Wheeler, and our neighbor, Trixie Belden." Then he gave Trixie the folder.

She spread it on her knees and stared at the neat handwriting. "Where do we start?" she whispered.

Honey looked over her shoulder and murmured, "You can skip that section on tools and household goods."

"And the description of their motor vehicles," added Jim.

"Let's see," Trixie mumbled. "A ten-year-old Dodge pickup . . . a late model Dodge compact . . . oh, here it is—livestock."

Trixie looked up and dropped her lashes at once. Roger Higgins was listening to every word they said. He shifted his position and then stood up to see what she was reading. When she tilted the paper, Roger walked over to stand behind her. Without being too obvious about it, she kept her arm covering as much of the page as she could. She didn't say a word when she found the section describing the black Shetland.

"Item number 204," Trixie murmured. She added nonchalantly, "Is the auction sales record here, too?"

"The kid's lookin' at it," Roger growled.

As Trixie glanced toward Jim for confirmation, Roger, pretending to be helpful, took the inventory folder from her hands. He took the sales record from Jim and then managed to spill the entire contents of the Dodge file on the floor. He scooped up the papers and did not return them.

"Who are you kids?" he demanded. "Why are you stickin' your noses into our business?" He tilted his can and drank noisily. "Frayne . . . Wheeler . . . Belden," he muttered. A light dawned. "From out near Glen Road somewhere?"

"Right," Jim said politely.

"Slumming, huh?" Roger's red, full lips moved halfway between a smile and a sneer. He drummed his fingers on his beer can and announced, "Okay, the party's over. Now get out."

"But—" Trixie protested.

Roger held open the screen door and made a sweeping bow. Hot with anger, Trixie had no choice except to go through the door and down the walk, followed first by Honey, then by Jim.

The minute they were back in the car, Trixie turned to Jim. "The pony—was it sold?"

"There's no record of a sale," Jim said as he hurried to get them safely out of the neighborhood.

"Good. That means Davy got his hands on him first," Trixie said. "If we find one, we'll find the other."

Jim looked at his watch. "We're late for lunch. Why don't we stop at Wimpy's?"

Both Honey and Trixie voted to go home. "Every minute that passes is moving us closer to nine o'clock," said Trixie.

"Besides, I feel uneasy about Dodgy since meeting Roger," Honey added apprehensively. "What if he follows us home?"

"He seemed to know where we live," Jim agreed.

"I wish he didn't," Trixie fretted.

"He could have checked our car license number," Jim said. "We were at his mercy."

As Jim drove up the farm lane, Trixie drew a deep breath. "Smell that bread! Come on in!"

"Just try to keep us out," Jim dared her.

Before the three could take more than a few steps away from the car, Bobby charged across the yard toward them, round-eyed and out of breath. "Just *guess* who's coming!" he shrieked.

175

Trixie looked where Bobby was pointing, unsure whether to be fearful or ecstatic. There, coming down the bicycle trail, was Brian on the handsome chestnut gelding, Starlight. Behind him was Dan riding Spartan, with Mart following on Strawberry, his favorite mount from the Wheeler stable. And behind them, led by a rope held by Mart, was a friendly, willing captive—a small, black, shaggy pony.

Since learning to ride Mr. Pony, Bobby considered himself to be an authority on ponies. "The littlest pony I ever did see" was his joyful comment.

"Where on earth—" began Trixie.

"Dan came over to help us with our chores," explained Brian, "and we finished in record time."

"So," Dan interrupted, "we decided to follow up on those tracks you found at Ten Acres. You people must not have looked closely enough last night, because—"

"Because," Mart concluded dramatically, "that is where our equestrian expedition reached a favorable termination, and our exploration evoked an ebony—"

"I can't listen to any more of this!" cried Trixie.

176

"I have to call Sergeant Molinson!"

The sergeant was properly impressed with the Bob-Whites' discovery. "Hang on to him," he ordered. "Davy will follow."

Trixie gulped. Now, how was she going to report about the trip to Sleepyside? Well, all she could do was tell him. So she did just that.

"*What?*" From the other end of the line, Trixie heard sounds decidedly like muffled curses. "I thought I asked *you* to search for the boy and the pony, while *I* looked for the crook!" he snapped.

"We didn't hunt crooks," Trixie said in a small voice, "just an auction clerk. I had to know more about Wicky."

"You could have asked Mrs. Dodge!" the sergeant roared.

"She isn't here. She went home last night," Trixie reported.

Words crackled into Trixie's ear. "This case is getting out of hand! I suppose *she* took the baby?"

"No, sir. Dodgy is here. Di's watching him."

"Well, see that *somebody* stays with him. I'm not sitting on my hands, you know! I've been doing some more checking on Roger Higgins.

177

A few weeks ago, he sat in on a poker game where the stakes were way over his head. Now that he's made the connection between the Dodge children and you, he may decide to pull something!"

"I—I know. That's what Honey was worried about," Trixie confessed miserably.

"Congratulate Honey for keeping her common sense!" the sergeant barked. "And keep in touch with me, y'hear? If the slightest thing goes wrong, call me!" *Bang* went the receiver.

What's Mutual? · 13

TRIXIE FELT LIKE A ROBOT in slow motion as she walked back to Honey. "The sergeant is mad," she said stiffly.

"How mad?" Honey asked, tears of sympathy welling.

"Plenty," Trixie admitted. "We'd better find Davy and get both those kids to the police station."

"How about some lunch first?" begged Mart.

"I'm famished," agreed Trixie. "Where are Moms and Dad?"

"Who cares?" Mart yelped, making a run for

the kitchen. "They left us fresh bread to make sandwiches!"

"They went over to the Dodges' to help them pack," said Brian. "And also to help them with errands, since the Dodges sold their cars."

"Dodgy was napping, so they left him here with me," Di put in proudly.

All the Bob-Whites got to work in the kitchen. Bobby wanted to share the excitement. " 'Member that sandwich I put on the doghouse?" he asked. "Well, you know what? Something ate it! I found the napkin on the ground behind the tool shed."

"Reddy probably picked it up and carried it back there to eat," Brian said, putting the finishing touches on his ham and cheese sandwich.

"No tooth marks on the napkin," Bobby chirped. "I looked."

Mart groaned loudly. "Methinks our youngest sibling doth create clamor like unto a shamus."

"Nope to whatever you said," retorted Bobby.

Trixie paused between bites of her peanut butter sandwich. "I think Bobby may have found a clue," she mused.

Bobby moved to sit beside the one who recognized his detective skills.

180

"Then why aren't we hunting?" Dan asked.

"Because the sergeant thinks Davy will follow the pony, and we're giving him a little time to do that before we start tearing the woods apart," Trixie said.

Bobby felt very important. "Know what else? I answered the phone a while ago. A man said he had a message about a pony from a mu-mutual friend named Moses White. I told him, 'Moses Bob White is our baby's name. What's mutual?' Then the man hung up!"

Jim, Trixie, and Honey heard that news with sinking hearts.

"Oh, I wish you hadn't said that," sighed Trixie. Then she related the morning's adventures, including the encounter with Roger Higgins, to the others. "That had to be Roger calling, and he's up to no good," she finished.

"Let's get going, then," urged Dan.

"Wait a second," Brian spoke up. "Moms demanded that Mart and I fix that washing machine before we do another thing this afternoon. The laundry's piled up to the ceiling, she says."

"And we Beldens will be forced to go au naturel soon," Mart added.

"Speak for yourself," said Trixie. "Oh, it's just

181

as well. Now we can go out in the yard and wait for Davy to show up."

"I'll fetch Dodgy," volunteered Di. "He could use some sun."

Brian and Mart went to work, and the other Bob-Whites gathered around Dodgy outside. Trixie leaned against a maple and anxiously watched the baby, who cooed in a friendly effort to talk to her. As worried as she was, she couldn't help giggling. "You little salamander," she teased.

Bobby dashed out of the house, swinging his jump rope. "Sit still," he hissed in Trixie's ear. "You're the kidnapper, and I'm gonna tie you up while I go find the police!"

"Okay, I surrender." Trixie's fright wasn't just for Bobby's benefit. She *was* feeling uneasy.

Clumsily but thoroughly, Bobby tied her to the tree. Then he raced away.

After a while, Trixie had to change position. The rope scraped the skin under her arms when she turned. A few seconds later, the same thing happened. She glanced down at the rope that Bobby had tied across her front, and her mental computer shifted gears. She tried to picture a boy, a baby, and a few supplies. It would be no small task to climb on a Shetland unless . . . "I know!" she yelled.

Honey looked concerned and rushed over to untie Bobby's knots. At once, Trixie ran toward the house, shouting, "Brian, I know how Dodgy got bruised!"

Brian came outside, wiping machine oil off his hands. Immediately Trixie scooped up Dodgy and asked Honey for the long, sheer scarf she was wearing to tie back her hair. Dodgy squeaked like a mouse.

"Trixie, Dodgy's not a rag doll, you know!" said Di, appalled.

Trixie flung the scarf into place under Dodgy's tiny bare arms. "Wait just a minute, Di. Here, take the baby, Brian, and pretend you have to get on a horse. You're not very tall, and you need both hands free. So you tie him to your own chest, and you climb up."

Brian whistled. "So Dodgy wasn't battered, after all. Davy was just trying to get organized. Poor baby." By this time, Dodgy was screaming. Brian cuddled him close to calm him.

"We keep saying 'poor baby,' " Trixie fretted. "But what about Davy? What a brave boy he must be! He tried so *hard* to take care of Dodgy.

What could have caused him to run away? What did his parents *do* to him?"

Honey was aghast. "Trixie, what are you talking about? Both of his parents seem kind and loving."

"How do we know what happens when doors are closed?" Trixie asked darkly. "Remember Davy's note? What made him think he was going to be sold? Who would cast away their children like they were, you know, old cars or something?" Then her mental computer clicked again. "*Cars!*" she shouted.

Everyone turned to look at her as though she had cracked up completely.

"Honey, Jim, don't you remember the inventory list?" Trixie rushed on. "They auctioned off two vehicles—an old Dodge and a new Dodge!"

"That's a coincidence," admitted Jim, "but so what?"

Honey jumped up in excitement. "The new Dodge," she breathed. "Eileen said that's why they called the baby Dodgy—because he's the new Dodge!"

"I see," Jim said. "So you think Davy ran away because he thought they were selling the baby, not the car. What could possibly make him believe something so weird?"

"I don't know, but it makes sense, doesn't it?" countered Trixie.

"I think it makes sense to let Dodgy get some rest," Di spoke up firmly.

"Right," said Brian, setting Dodgy back down on his blanket. "Oh, I'm sorry. I knew I'd get oil on him."

Trixie smacked her brow with her palm. "Of course," she said with sudden understanding. "There was machine oil as well as tar at that old Dutch barn. There was even alfalfa. And Davy had been washing Dodgy's clothes without soap in the spring across the road."

"Well, so much for the clues Dodgy brought with him," said Brian.

Just then, Mart loped into the yard and tossed a grease-smeared pin into Trixie's lap. "The culprit!" he announced dramatically.

Bobby followed behind Mart, saying, "That's the biggest safety pin I ever saw."

"It's a horse's blanket pin, that's why," Dan pointed out.

"From the fly sheet!" exclaimed Trixie and Honey at the same time.

"Davy must have used it for Dodgy's diaper

185

after he left the fly sheet at the inn," Honey went on.

"Smart little Davy," moaned Trixie.

And not-so-smart little Trixie, she thought with disgust. Fine detective she was—practically leading a kidnapper to helpless children and finding clues no longer needed!

Before she could lecture herself any more, there was a sudden screech of tires in the driveway. The group on the lawn looked up to see a red sports car, with the top down, coming to a halt not far from them. The driver had a moustache and a bushy brown beard.

"Roger Higgins!" Trixie gasped. She instinctively moved closer to Dodgy.

"I do declare!" Roger called. He leaned back and spread an arm along the back of the car seat. "I'm returning your little visit. Polite of me, huh? I thought we might have a chat with our mutual friend, Moses White." His glance swung from Dodgy to the pony that browsed near the fence. "But I see you already have company. I'll just have to come back another time!"

He spun his car around, the wheels kicking up gravel, and left as quickly as he had come.

"What's mutual?" Bobby wanted to know.

Trixie was so angry and frightened that she couldn't answer.

"Two people feeling or doing the same thing at the same time," explained Brian.

"Then I mutual that guy," Bobby said. "I don't like him, same as he doesn't like us."

"Me, too, Bobby," Trixie said. "I don't mutual that man." Then she pounded her bare knees with both fists. "Oh, what are we to do? He saw both Dodgy and Wicky, and he must think Davy's here, too. We *can't* wait for Davy to come in on his own, even though the sergeant thinks he will."

"Did he give us a direct order to wait?" Honey asked.

When Trixie's sandy curls shook, Dan got to his feet. "We've waited long enough then," he declared.

Leaving Dan and Di behind to protect Dodgy, the others began a thorough scouring of the grounds around Crabapple Farm.

Even Bobby joined in the search, staying as close as he could to Mart. Trixie chose the woods area nearest the doghouse. She shouted her throat raw in calling for Davy, but there was never a sound to be heard except the same calls from the other Bob-Whites.

In the early dusk, the group met in the kitchen, tired, hungry, and discouraged. They fixed more sandwiches and shared their findings.

Brian had noticed several apple cores in the orchard. Jim held up a shoelace that nobody claimed. Mart presented Jim's beach towel, which Honey and Trixie recalled seeing at the boat-house.

"Well, I found it on the flat roof of the chicken house, behind the tool shed," Mart said.

"That's where I found the napkin," Bobby put in. "And where I found this!" He thrust forward a carrot top with only a rim of orange left below the greenery.

"The towel was folded into a mattress," said Mart. "He must have slept here last night."

Trixie was so tired that tears seemed to be the only relief. "It's all my fault," she wailed. "I should never have gone near those auctioneers!" Then she straightened up in her chair. "I almost forgot—the sergeant said to call him if anything went wrong. I guess it's time to call."

This time, the sergeant didn't roar when Trixie explained the latest developments. "Okay, now listen to me," he commanded. "I'm calling your parents to have them bring the Dodges here. And I want all of you to pile into that station wagon of yours and bring the baby to the police station. Don't leave *anybody* at the farm who might be held as a hostage. It seems that Roger Higgins chose the worst possible company for his poker game. They were all ex-cons from the state penitentiary. Roger owes money to one named Sax Jenner, who got out last month. So just do what I say, and don't waste any time about it."

"But what about Davy?" Trixie blurted.

"I have men looking for him. Now, move!"

Trixie hung up and relayed the sergeant's orders to the others. They immediately stopped eating and started getting ready to go. Trixie raced to her room to get a jacket. On her way up the stairs, she glanced back through the open door of the guest room.

She shouted to the red T-shirt bending over Dodgy's basket, "Bobby, don't try to lift Dodgy! Brian will carry him." As she reached the top of the stairs, she heard the slam of the downstairs bathroom door. Jacket in hand, she ran back down the stairs and met Brian in the hall, with Dodgy in his arms.

"Everybody else is in the wagon," he told her.

" 'Cept me," Bobby said. He went to the refrigerator for the baby's next bottle and snatched up a box of diapers from the counter. The last one into the Bob-White station wagon, he slid into the front seat next to Trixie.

Jim drove as fast as he could without going over the speed limit. They had made it as far as the outskirts of Sleepyside, when headlights blinded Jim briefly. The lights dazzled Trixie's eyes, too. Beside her, Bobby's T-shirt was a white blob.

"Idiot!" Jim muttered.

Brian twisted in his seat and said, "That looked like—"

"I know. That red job of Roger Higgins's," Jim said, glancing into his rearview mirror.

Red.

Jim had said "red"!

Suddenly Trixie turned to Bobby. "When did you change your T-shirt?"

"Before lunch," Bobby said. "Moms made me."

"But it isn't red!" Trixie said.

"It never was," Bobby retorted.

"Are you sure?"

"Sure, I'm sure. It's my T-shirt!"

"What is this—" Brian began.

"Turn around, Jim!" Trixie yelled.

The others swiveled their heads toward her.

"Trixie!" Mart exploded.

"I thought the sergeant said to come straight to the station," Honey said, her voice rising in alarm.

"And," Trixie shouted, "he said not to leave anybody in the house who could be taken as hostage, and Davy Dodge is in our house!"

Hostages! • 14

Surrounded by shocked silence, Trixie lowered her voice to a whisper. "Please—I saw him there," she pleaded.

"Okay," Jim sighed. He swung into a driveway, backed out, and started toward the farm. "Something tells me we should go to the station first, then to the farm, but—"

"Hurry!" croaked Trixie.

"Look up there," Dan said. "Looks like Higgins was turning around to come after us."

Sure enough, the red sports car had pulled into a driveway. The minute Jim passed it, however, it moved back onto the road, accelerating to catch up to the station wagon.

"He's following us!" Honey gasped.

Jim increased his speed. Dodgy broke into a fretful whimpering.

From the backseat of the Bob-White station wagon, Mart said sharply, "Watch it, Jim. Those headlights are coming up on us awfully fast."

"I know," Jim said tensely. "I've been trying to shake him, but he just hangs in there." He gritted his teeth. "He's got us trapped!"

Suddenly the whole interior of the wagon was flooded with light that blazed into Jim's eyes. "Shift that mirror!" he snapped at Trixie.

Trixie obeyed, watching those freckled hands on the steering wheel and praying silently. *If anyone can get us out of this nightmare, Jim can. . . .*

"Don't slow down," warned Brian. "He can't miss hitting us."

"I'm sorry, gang," said Jim, his voice cracking a little. "All I can do is stay on the road and hope I have time to make the turn at the mailbox. Hang on, everyone!"

He negotiated a curve in the road, sending gravel flying but still managing to keep the car upright. Brian doubled over to shield Dodgy more effectively.

"If ever we needed Sergeant Molinson to check my speed, this is the time," Jim muttered.

"There's the mailbox," Trixie said as she wrapped her arms around Bobby and braced herself for the turn into the farm lane.

Jim clenched the steering wheel tighter and, without braking, swerved into the lane. The red car shot past, still on Glen Road. Jim immediately slammed on the brakes.

"Watch it, Jim!" Mart complained loudly.

"You want me to kill that kid?" Jim yelled back.

Trixie gulped down her fright and raised her head. The long black tail of the Shetland was so close to the station wagon that she couldn't believe Jim had missed hitting him. A small figure wearing a red T-shirt was sliding off the pony and making a dash for the bushes.

Without another word, Jim leaped out of his seat and dragged the boy, kicking and screaming, back to the car.

As Jim shoved him into the front seat, the boy cried, "I wasn't stealing Wicky, honest I wasn't. He's mine!"

"It's okay, Davy," Trixie said. "Just stay put. We have to get you to the police station. Come on, Jim! Let's get out of here!"

"It's too late," Jim announced grimly, watching his rearview mirror.

The others swiveled around in time to see the red sports car careening into the lane behind them.

"Now we're really trapped!" wailed Di.

As the red car jerked to a halt, a bulky figure hurtled out of the driver's seat and rushed toward the darkness of the house. A second, smaller figure approached the Bob-Whites' car.

"Lock your doors, everyone," urged Trixie.

A man with a face Trixie had never seen peered through the window of the station wagon. "Into the house, kids," he ordered, tapping the glass with a gun. "Very slowly. Don't pull any fancy tricks. And give me those car keys."

The group had no choice but to obey. With her heart knocking the breath from her throat, Trixie grabbed Bobby's hand. She saw Mart reach for Davy's. Brian's strong arms were wrapped around Dodgy. Cautiously the group began its way to the porch.

Trixie had a flashing impression of movement.

After an instant of panic, she realized that Jim had disappeared. *Where could he be?* she thought wildly. Then she remembered his ten-speed, still leaning against the porch.

As Trixie stumbled forward, her mind worked desperately on the problem of escaping without endangering lives, but for the moment, she pinned her faith on Jim. Jim had headlights on his ten-speed, and he knew every twist and turn of that bicycle path. In daylight, his downhill speed had been clocked at forty-five miles per hour.

Unless he was upset by a wandering porcupine or a startled deer, he would reach the telephone at Glen Road Inn in a matter of minutes.

"You're hurting my hand," Bobby mumbled.

"We have to stick together," Trixie told him.

Finally the group entered the Belden kitchen. The light flashed on, and the young people instinctively gathered around the baby, who looked ready to scream any minute.

The man with the gun followed them in and surveyed the room. "Well, well, well," he said in a voice that sounded almost friendly. "What have we here?"

Trixie had figured out that this must be Sax

Jenner, the ex-convict the sergeant had mentioned. He was short and slim and deceptively handsome. Roger Higgins appeared in the doorway, and Sax turned on him, demanding, "Where's that redheaded kid?"

"Who cares?" Roger retorted. "I just happened to bump into some bicycle tires with my knife."

Trixie's heart sank.

"Jim can ride a horse!" Bobby piped up. Quickly Trixie clamped her hand over Bobby's unshushable mouth.

Roger winked at Bobby. "Those horses out there by the fence looked kind of lonesome," he said, "so I opened the gate and sent them home."

Trixie caught her breath. Oh, well. Surely Regan would know that something was wrong when those valuable animals returned home at this hour of the night without any riders. Maybe he would call the police. Anyway, maybe Jim had managed to get away in Brian's jalopy.

Just then, Roger threw a sly look at Sax. "I also got rid of the gas in the jalopy," he said. "I've been a busy boy, you know." He tossed Sax the car keys. "Now it's your turn to get busy," he said.

Sax twirled his gun, an evil smirk on his face.

197

"Think you'll need the persuader?"

"Depends on your plan," Roger answered warily. It was obvious to Trixie that Roger didn't particularly want to handle the gun.

Sax pretended to consider the problem, but Trixie sensed that he knew exactly what he was going to do. His voice made him seem friendly, but those eyes were as cold as snake eyes. Finally he announced, "We're going to get that Dodge money, one way or another. All we were going to do was hold on to those two Dodge kids, but now—well, now we've got a chance to raise a whole hunk of money from the parents of all these kids!"

Trixie saw Brian's arms tremble at Sax's threat.

Sax grinned boldly at Roger. "In other words, we have to keep this bunch under control, don't we? It'll be simple!" With a quick change of mood, he stalked across the kitchen and poked the gun at Bobby's chest. Coldly he told Trixie, "Turn loose of that hand, sis, or he's had it."

"Y-You'll have to kill me, too!" Trixie said, clutching Bobby's hand even tighter. She could hear moaning sounds coming from Bobby. She glanced down and saw that he wasn't crying. Bobby Belden was angry.

"I don't mutual you!" Bobby yelled as he kicked Sax in the shins.

"Don't make him mad, Bobby!" begged Trixie.

"I can handle the kid—it's you that's making me mad, sis," Sax sneered. "Let go of him."

Trixie obeyed.

"I gotta go to the bathroom!" Bobby roared.

Sax looked disgusted. "Take him," he told Roger, "but make it snappy."

While Bobby and Roger were out of the room, Sax's snake eyes flicked from one face to another. When he noticed Mart's hand inching toward the knife rack on the wall, Sax warned silkily, "Don't bother, kid."

"Oh, Mart, keep your temper," Di pleaded.

"You'd better ask *him* to do the same, Di," muttered Dan. "This little man has seen too many shoot-'em-ups."

For the first time, Sax's anger flared. "Higgins!" he shouted. "Bring that kid back here so I can get going!"

Bobby caused as much commotion as possible when Roger dragged him back to the kitchen, and Dodgy began to wail.

"Look what you did!" Davy shrieked at Sax.

"I'm sorry," said Sax with mock concern. "But

199

I must be on my way. I'm receiving a donation of twenty thousand beautiful green ones!" He picked up Bobby's jump rope, which was hanging over the back of a chair. Sax tossed the rope to Roger, who started to tie Bobby's hands behind his back.

"Put it around his neck," Sax suggested, "so you can jerk it if anybody gets a brainstorm about tackling you."

Roger looped the jump rope around Bobby's neck, a smile showing between his beard and moustache. "While I'm here, I'll start writing the notes to their daddies. They were so polite about bringing one to mine!"

"You do that," Sax said. His gun in one hand, he saluted smartly with the other and stepped backward through the screen door, grinning from ear to ear.

Then, to everyone's amazement, Sax twitched as though he'd received an electric shock, and his grin changed to a look of dismay.

A familiar voice, coming from behind Sax, barked, "Drop that gun!"

The weapon clattered to the floor as Sax's hands shot into the air and were immediately fastened with handcuffs.

Roger Higgins looked as though he couldn't decide whether to reach for the gun on the floor or to try to escape into the rest of the house. As his grasp tightened on the rope around Bobby's neck, Sergeant Molinson and another police officer stormed into the kitchen. An instant later, Roger's hands were also handcuffed.

Dizzy with relief, Trixie rushed to Bobby and hugged his sturdy body. While the others followed her example, Davy pulled on Brian's sleeve.

"Please let me touch Dodgy," Davy said shyly.

Brian sat down in a kitchen chair and held out the crying baby. Davy laid his cheek against the baby's and crooned, "Oh, Dodgy, I've missed you. Don't cry—you're safe now."

Trixie gulped when Dodgy stopped crying. The baby seemed to recognize Davy's voice and touch. *This* was what she had been working for— the reuniting of a family.

The sergeant held out a big solid hand to Trixie. She placed hers in it for a bone-crunching handshake.

Trixie put an arm around Davy's shoulders. She said, "This is Davy Dodge."

The sergeant bent down to shake Davy's hand,

too. "Am I glad to meet you!" he said gruffly.

"Where's Jim?" Trixie asked suddenly.

"I told you we should have kept track of that redheaded kid!" Sax growled at Roger.

Sergeant Molinson ordered both handcuffed men to sit down and keep quiet. Then he turned back to Trixie. "We passed Jim on the road," he said. "He waved us on. He looked beat. I knew something was wrong when you people didn't show up at the station like you were supposed to. Seeing Jim alone on Glen Road confirmed my suspicion, and we got over here as fast as we could."

Even as the sergeant was explaining, Jim walked in through the screen door. He glistened with perspiration and was so tired that Trixie could count each freckle on his face. When Jim saw the handcuffed men, his green eyes blazed with fierce pride. "We did it again, gang!" he panted.

"Thank you, Jim," Trixie said. "Thank you, James Winthrop Frayne."

"You are welcome, Beatrix Belden," Jim said quietly.

"Only my dad says Beatrix," Bobby put in.

"And f-friends who risk their necks for you,"

Trixie corrected Bobby shakily.

Right behind Jim came Mr. and Mrs. Belden and Eileen and David Dodge.

"Are you kids all right?" Peter shouted.

"Our boys, David! *Both* our boys!" Eileen choked. Her shaking arms enveloped Davy, while David's hands reached instantly for Dodgy.

"I promised myself I wouldn't cry," Eileen sobbed, "and here I am."

"You're entitled to tears, Eileen," the sergeant said gently.

Trixie looked around. The only dry eyes in the room belonged to Roger and Sax, and they were staring straight ahead. Trixie couldn't help scowling at the prisoners. Sax returned the stare coldly, but Roger looked embarrassed. Trixie decided that Roger was really more of a weakling than a criminal.

"It's time to clear up some things," the sergeant decided.

"Don't look at me," Sax said. "I didn't take those kids."

"Me neither," Roger said. His hands were locked together, but he didn't seem to know what to do with his feet. He shuffled them awkwardly.

"We're not talking about taking kids," said

the sergeant. "We're talking about making threats!"

"Oh, that." Sax's eyes were bold. "Is there a law against typewriting?"

"There is when it's a ransom note," the sergeant snapped back. "Just what was it that inspired you?"

Sax jerked his head at Roger. "Talk to him."

Roger Higgins had decided that his feet fitted together best when they were ankle to ankle. He hunched his shoulders up around his ears, his great brush of brown hair sticking out like a clown's wig.

"Well?" the sergeant barked, cupping one ear.

"Okay, okay," Roger said. "We was taking inventory out at the Dodge farm. That is, my pop was, and I was just hanging around. I'm supposed to be learning the business."

"You *were* learning the business," the sergeant corrected him.

Roger nodded at Davy, who was leaning against his father's shoulder. "There was this kid following us around, listening to everything we said. I could see he wasn't liking it one bit. He just about had a fit when Pop wrote down the description of his pony. But his daddy tried to tell him how it had to go 'cause they couldn't keep no livestock in the apartment they were moving to.

"And I winked at his daddy, and I asked, 'How much are you askin' for your kids?' And he winked back and said, 'How much do you think they'll bring?' "

"David!" Eileen gasped in horror. "You *said* that?"

David bit his lips and nodded. "So that's what you meant in your note about selling you and the baby," he said, handing Dodgy to Eileen and giving Davy an enormous hug.

Roger went on. "Then the kid sort of tugged his daddy's sleeve and said, 'You can sell me if you have to, but not the new Dodge.' That didn't make much sense, but I could see the kid was hurtin' bad, and he wasn't in any mood for teasing.

"Then pretty soon we got to the implement shed, and there was this new car standing there."

"A Dodge compact," Trixie recalled.

Roger traded scowls with Trixie. "When we got there, my pop asked, 'You're sure about the new Dodge?' The kid's daddy said, 'I've got my back to the wall. I can't afford to feed an extra cat, so everything goes.' Well, that kid took off like a shot. Later, I saw him ride off on the pony with the baby. He wasn't seen hide nor hair of till this—" At a loss for words, Roger glared at Trixie.

"The word is girl," Mart informed him.

"—*girl* stuck her nose into my business!"

"Just what made it your business?" the sergeant asked.

"Why not?" Roger Higgins flared. "Sax was crowding me for the five thousand dollars I owed him. I told him about the kids disappearing, and he came up with the idea of collecting ransom from the kids' daddy. That way, we'd both make a profit. We had no idea where the silly kids were, but Sax said we should write the first note anyway. Then we looked around for the kids but couldn't find 'em. So Sax made me up the ante to twenty thousand and write the second note."

"You knew how much the Dodges would make at their auction, and you asked for all of it," Trixie accused.

"Sure, why not?" Roger was unrepentant.

"So it would end up in Sax's pocket?" the sergeant asked.

"So what?" Roger yelled. "It let me off the hook!" He had a slow wit, but Trixie suspected it was finally dawning on him that breaking a law had put him in worse trouble than owing money.

In the crowded farmhouse kitchen, a small voice was heard. "I didn't know those men wrote notes to my daddy," said Davy Dodge.

"Why did you take your baby brother and run away?" the sergeant asked gently.

Davy's lips quivered. "They told you. Daddy was going to sell the new Dodge and Wicky and me because he couldn't afford to keep us. I—I guess he didn't mean the baby, after all."

David held Davy close and said, "I'm sorry, son. I thought you understood I was joking."

"When someone's hurting, you don't make jokes, Mr. Dodge," said Jim, a former runaway himself.

Quietly David answered, "I guess I was hurting, too, so I tried to joke my way through losing the farm."

"Oh, Davy, how did you manage?" his mother cried.

"I took some bottles and diapers, and I took Wicky's fly sheet so I could take care of him, too.

207

I broke my piggy bank and Dodgy's, but he didn't have much in his. I didn't have room to take anything else, so I guess you sold my clothes and books and toys, huh?"

"Of course not, Davy," Eileen assured him. "We even kept that clock you like so much."

"Then what did you do, Davy?" the sergeant prompted.

"Well, I had trouble getting on Wicky with Dodgy, so I used the fly sheet to tie Dodgy against me as tight as I could, so I wouldn't drop him. I had to do that every time I climbed on Wicky. Sometimes, I—I bumped Dodgy and he cried." Davy reached out to touch his brother, who had fallen asleep in his mother's arms.

"He cried when I stuck him with the pin, too. He cried an awful lot, but I tried to take care of him, honest I did! I was scared, though. There were lots of highways.

"When we got across all those highways, I was glad to get into the woods. Only it was lots bigger than I thought it was. Wicky lost one of his shoes, so I borrowed some tools and took his other shoes off. I found a good place to stay, where some men fed me out of their lunch pails, and I milked a goat named Nancy. But Dodgy got so he didn't wake up much, and he didn't want to drink his milk.

"He liked to be clean, so I washed his diapers in a brook and dried them on the bushes, but I had to chase Wicky part of the time. Wicky liked to play with Nancy at the barn. Once I saw that man." Davy pointed a shaky finger at Roger. "I thought he was hunting for us to sell us, so I took a man's T-shirt and tore it up to make diapers, 'cause Dodgy's weren't dry yet. Then we rode some more.

"When it got dark that day, we slept under a bush at a kind of hotel. I had a hard time keeping track of things. I kept losing stuff, like diapers and bootees and bottles and the fly sheet. One night it got very hot and thundery. I knew it was going to storm. I tried to build a tepee, but it was too small for me and Dodgy, so I just kept going.

"Then I saw this doghouse. There was no dog in it, so I just put Dodgy in to keep him dry till the rain stopped. Only—only then I couldn't get him back!"

By this time, Davy was sobbing. Both parents patted and cuddled him as if they would never be able to touch him enough in a lifetime. It seemed to Trixie that, as careless as the Dodges might have previously been with their money, they could never be as careless with their love for their sons.

Davy rubbed his eyes and continued. "Wicky and me found plenty of places to sleep in the woods, but I tried to stay as close to Dodgy as I could. I knew Dodgy would be safe here in case that man was still hunting for us. This house is easy to get into. People go in and out all the time and leave doors open."

The shadows and sounds . . . the misplaced rug and the mud . . . the open refrigerator . . . *Of course*, thought Trixie. *Davy's been watching over Dodgy just like Miriam kept watch over her brother Moses in his basket.*

"Sometimes the dog barked at me," Davy went on, "but no one else seemed to know I was here."

"What did you have to eat, son?" his father asked.

"There's a garden and an orchard on this farm," Davy explained. "I pulled up stuff—just what I needed," he added hastily, looking apologetically at the Beldens. "Once I took food from the refrigerator, but I paid for it!"

"I found your money," Di put in.

"And I gave you a sandwich," Bobby added, feeling important.

"It was a good sandwich," Davy said. After a silence, he asked his father, "Did you get enough money, Daddy? Do you still have to sell us?" He bit his lower lip to keep it from shaking.

"We *weren't* going to sell you, and we never will," David said earnestly, kissing his son's forehead.

"We aren't going to an apartment," his mother told him. "Your daddy has a new job. He'll be working on a farm, and we'll be living on the farm with him."

"Wicky, too?" Davy asked.

"Of course," Eileen said.

Bobby looked crestfallen at the idea of losing a pony that he had known so short a time, but then he brightened. "I'll come see you, Davy."

"We'll both ride Wicky," Davy offered.

"But Dodgy'll have to wait till he's big like us," Bobby said. "I don't think he likes to be tied up."

Trixie took the coins from the top of the refrigerator and handed some to Davy. "You paid us too much," she told him. "We also found some of your money in the woods."

211

"I knew I lost some when I took a bath," Davy said.

It all fits together, Trixie thought. *Even the soap.*

At that moment, the telephone rang. The call was for Jim.

"Yes, Regan," said Jim. "I know Starlight, Strawberry, and Spartan came home with a Shetland. I hoped they did, at any rate. Will you please send someone to pick up Honey and me?"

Jim winked at the group gathered around him in the kitchen. "Why do we need a ride? Well, I'll tell you, Regan. Brian's gas tank is empty. The tires on my ten-speed are slashed. A police car, a red convertible, and the Beldens' car are blocking the way of the Bob-White station wagon in the lane. It's getting pretty crowded around here, so it's time we all clear out. That's why we need a ride!"

"You don't need to go, Jim," Bobby said. "Our walls are stretchy. Moms says so."

Eileen Dodge shifted the weight of the baby in her arms and said tremulously, "And so are your hearts."

"We Dodges owe *all* of you a debt we can never repay," her husband agreed.

212

Di's violet eyes sparkled impishly. "You and your family can pay *me* back by coming to my party tomorrow," she said.

"What party?" teased Mart. "Jeepers! We know who Dodgy is—he doesn't need a naming ceremony anymore."

"We're having the party because I've already done all the preparations for it!" Di retorted.

"And besides," added Trixie, kissing the top of Dodgy's downy head, "look how much more than just a name we have to celebrate now!"

Dodgy awoke, stretched his arms, and cooed his agreement.